10648729

Also by K. Ancrum

The Wicker King

THE WEIGHT OF THE STARS

K. ANCRUM

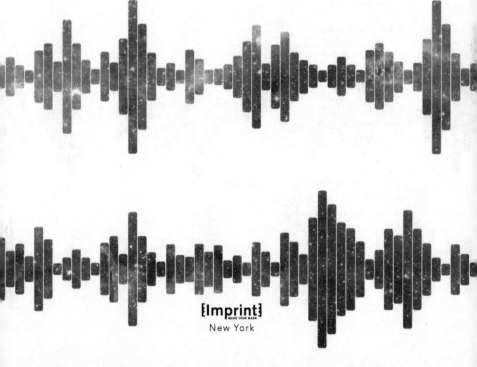

[Imprint]
MAKE YOUR MARK

New York

[Imprint]
MAKE YOUR MARK

A part of Macmillan Publishing Group, LLC
175 Fifth Avenue, New York, NY 10010

Sources: p. 362, *Gizmodo* guest blog; p. 364, NPR interview; p. 365, ScienceBlogs
.com interview; p. 366, Reddit post; p. 367, *How We Live* article; p. 368, *Air &
Space Magazine*; p. 369, *Spaceman: An Astronaut's Unlikely Journey to Unlock
the Secrets of the Universe*; p. 370, Scholastic interview

Library of Congress Control Number: 2018936704

ISBN 978-1-250-10163-1 (hardcover) / ISBN 978-1-250-10164-8 (ebook)

Our books may be purchased in bulk for promotional, educational, or business
use. Please contact your local bookseller or the Macmillan Corporate and Premium
Sales Department at (800) 221-7945 ext. 5442 or by email at MacmillanSpecial
Markets@macmillan.com.

Book design by Ellen Duda
Imprint logo designed by Amanda Spielman

First edition, 2019

10 9 8 7 6 5 4 3 2 1

fiercereads.com

We are all dust just waiting to return to dust.
Treat this book kindly as you would yourself,
Because when our sun burns all into one, it will be.

This book is for all of us who looked up at the sky in wonder, and then cried when we learned how much calculus separated us from the stars.

Ten million light-years from now
bathed in the radiation of a time without time
are the bones of a girl who loved Ryann Bird.
≠
In the dust left over from our supernova
atoms spread farther and wider than hope
are pieces of the heart of the girl who
loved Alexandria the Great.

DAWN

She woke up to the sound of screaming.

She *always* woke up to the sound of screaming. Ryann scrunched her eyes against it for a minute and then rubbed her face in exhaustion. Eventually, she heaved herself from bed and lumbered into the living room.

"Hey, *heyheyhey*," she whispered. "It's okay."

She picked up Charlie and put him in his rocker on the floor, tipping it gently back and forth with her foot as she opened the fridge.

Her younger brother, James, was still snoring loudly a couple of rooms over, but she waited until Charlie was clean and fed to pop her head in and wake him up.

"Get up, it's six forty-five."

James just sighed and flopped over.

"Seriously, James." Ryann pushed herself into James's room, kicking dirty clothes and magazines out of the way. She yanked his dresser open and pulled out a pair of torn jeans and a black T-shirt and tossed them on James's bed.

"I'm leaving in ten minutes." She slammed the door shut behind her.

15 MINUTES

Ryann wiped Charlie's face clean and buttoned him up into his cold-weather onesie. She packed the baby some food and then dropped him off with their neighbor Ms. Worthing.

By the time she got back, James was awake, dressed, and smoking on the front stairs.

"Did you eat yet?" she asked.

He stared at Ryann blankly, eyes bleary with exhaustion. His purple hair was a tangled nest. Ryann sighed in exasperation and went back inside so that she could grab some granola bars and her leather jacket.

She tossed one bar into his lap on her way out and hopped onto her motorcycle. Ryann waited patiently until she felt James sluggishly climb on behind her and put his arms loosely around her waist. Then she took off up the highway to the next town over.

The Bird siblings had had many good things snatched from them.

Their father had been a handyman with a small business and loyal clients. He'd had a big red beard and large hands and a laugh that echoed over fields and hills. Their mother had been a mathematician working for NASA. They loved their wild tall girl and small round boy as best they could. But, one bright morning, they died. Sometimes, people just die.

A little while afterward, James stopped talking altogether. Then, a year later he brought a baby home. A baby with red hair, owlish eyes, and a laugh that echoed. Ryann had questions, but James never answered them. And like on that terrible bright morning a year before, she swallowed hard, tightened her shoelaces, and stood up to meet it.

So there they were:

Sitting in the ruins of the best that they could build.

And it would always have to be enough.

45 MINUTES

There was a larger town near the one Ryann Bird lived in. Ryann drove them miles to get there every morning.

It didn't have a trailer park where girls could live, snug with their little brother and his baby. Or a Laundromat where most of the machines were broken. Or a big parking lot that was supposed to become a grocery store, but didn't.

This town had a school and a mall and the sort of families who made sure both kids ate their breakfast before they left the house. Who drove them to school in luxury cars and made sure they had school supplies.

It was the best in the district. They were lucky it was that close.

Ryann tucked her bike behind the school in the lot where teachers liked to park. James hopped off, smacked her on the shoulder in thanks, and ran to class. Ryann swung her bookbag over her shoulder and walked slowly into the building.

10 MINUTES

Ryann was always late, so she didn't bother to hurry. She used to run to get to her seat, but none of the teachers ever gave her a break so she just figured, why even bother?

She knew what she looked like, and she looked like trouble. So she was nearly always in it regardless of the circumstances.

Ryann had been trimming her wild black hair herself since junior year and it showed. After the bright morning accident, she had a deep scar on one cheekbone, and no matter how much concealer she used, nothing ever quite hid it. Then, to make things worse, she'd become so exhausted and red-eyed since Charlie arrived that she kept getting accused of being high even though she didn't even smoke. She looked meaner and harder than she had any business looking at this nice rich school in this nice rich neighborhood. So she just became what she looked like. It was easier than fighting it.

Ryann slammed the door open and walked in, passing right in front of the room, obscuring the light of the projector.

"Always a pleasure, Ryann," Mrs. Marsh, their history teacher, drawled sarcastically.

Ryann trudged to a chair in the back of the room. She dropped her bookbag on the floor, then tapped the kid in front of her on the back to ask for a pencil. Jefferson, who sat in front of her most of the time and generally had loads of pencils, waved his empty pencil case. He reached forward and tapped the girl in front of him on the shoulder.

"Hey. Ryann Bird needs a pencil."

The girl didn't even turn around. She just sat ramrod straight in her chair and said very quietly. "Ryann can bring her own pencils to school. Just like everyone else."

It was deafeningly quiet. Mrs. Marsh cleared her throat meaningfully.

"Any student who needs a pencil can get one from the pencil jar on the front of my desk." she said, looking at Ryann pointedly.

Ryann got up, went to the front of the room, and grabbed a few.

As she walked back to her desk, she reached out and let her fingertips glide over the top of the desk of the girl who'd denied her. As gentle and silent as a promise.

Their town was small. New residents couldn't escape scrutiny if they tried, but this was definitely the first time Ryann had seen this girl at her school. Even so, Ryann couldn't quite shake the feeling that she was familiar somehow.

She hadn't been called on in class at all, so Ryann didn't know her name. She was brand-new, so it wasn't like Ryann could look her up on Facebook by looking up mutual friends from school and scouring their network for her name.

And she looked different.

She was at least half black—which was rare here. This town was unfortunately pretty homogenous.

She had very short bleached-blond hair and severe, thunderous eyebrows. Her mouth had been tight and angry looking—which was rich because she was the one being rude.

Ryann stared at the back of the girl's head and tapped her pencil against the side of her desk.

12 MINUTES

The bell rang. Ryann shoved her things back into her book-bag and rushed toward the door.

"Miss Bird, can I see you for a minute?"

A wave of exhaustion and irritation swept over her, but Ryann turned around to face her history teacher.

"Come wait by my desk."

Mrs. Marsh wiped off the projector and cleared the white-board while the rest of the students filed out. When the last person besides Ryann had gone, she closed the door.

She settled back down at her desk and pushed a small stack of worksheets to the side. "I have a favor to ask you."

"Will I get extra credit?" Ryann crossed her arms and stared down at Mrs. Marsh.

"Hmmm ... maybe I'll round up when we do a bell curve."

Ryann nodded. "Continue."

"As you noticed, we have a new student with us. Her name is Alexandria Macallough."

"Rude girl, won't make direct eye contact?" Ryann asked.

"Yes. Now, I know that normally a request like this wouldn't come to someone like you naturally, but it would be a huge help if you could look after her a bit. She's going to have some difficulty adjusting and making friends here, and from

8

what I can see, you have a bit of a track record for reaching out to people like that. Plus with the circumstances—"

"What circumstances?" Ryann interrupted.

Mrs. Marsh explained further. Ryann nodded and relaxed a bit as she listened.

"That's different," she said when Mrs. Marsh finished. "I thought you were going to ask me something else. But yeah, it's no problem. I'll see if I can get her to open up."

"I'm sorry. This is such a difficult circumstance for me. I've never had to assign someone to befriend someone else before," Mrs. Marsh admitted. "But I just felt like you might be the only person who could reach out in a way that would work."

Ryann snorted. "Well, that's flattering. Are you going to want to check in with me about it?"

"Maybe every few weeks or so. It's important, but not so important that we need to meet every day," Mrs. Marsh said.

"Hmm." Ryann crossed her arms again and thought about it for a bit.

"I would really appreciate it and I'm sure Alexandria would, too," Mrs. Marsh said softly.

Ryann's phone buzzed in her pocket, so she whipped it out. Her best friend, Ahmed, had texted a bunch of question marks. She sent back a single exclamation point.

"I've gotta go, but we've got a deal. If you don't want to do regular meetings, I'll just swing by after class if I have any questions or updates." Ryann walked over to the door, but stopped right before stepping through it. "And thanks for the bell curve leniency." She smirked.

Mrs. Marsh rolled her eyes. "Yeah, yeah, you're welcome. Go to your next class before I have to write you a pass."

2 HOURS AND 15 MINUTES

Ahmed Bateman, Ryann's best friend, was ten times what anyone expected him to be. He was beautiful, with black eyes and black hair that he wound up tightly into his navy blue turban. His face was angular, but pretty, and he was a bit on the shorter side.

He looked like his parents. Like all three of them. Two dads and one mom.

They showed up to report-card pickups and school events shamelessly, all three, hand in hand. There were ghosts of them all over Ahmed, to the point where it was impossible to ask who fathered Ahmed without being savagely impolite and overly specific.

Ryann liked Ahmed because weathering that had made him tough, but living it had made him sweet. A winning combination, which prompted Ahmed to decide it was a great idea to backhand Thompson when he called Ryann a dyke when they were in fifth grade—even though he and Ryann had never spoken to each other before.

They'd been close ever since. No one but James knew her better.

So when Ryann texted Ahmed that exclamation point, he knew to gather the others so they all could discuss something important.

2 CLASS PERIODS

A little past the baseball diamonds, behind the building, there was a huge hill. There were a lot of places to meet in the city, but this was the only one close enough to get to between classes without shirking the entire day.

Shannon, Blake, Tomas, and James were already waiting for Ahmed and Ryann at the top.

Shannon was exceptionally popular, but Blake and Tomas were a year younger, juniors like James. They'd both opted to be a bit more alternative than was considered appropriate—Tomas, gangly and tall with his bright red Mohawk, and Blake who shaved his head and had been giving himself stick-and-poke tattoos since middle school. They didn't have anyone else to be with, so Ryann had gathered them beneath her wing.

"There's a new kid!" Ahmed hollered up the hill.

"Really?!" Tomas shouted back. "Are you sure someone didn't just get a bad haircut?"

"NO!" Ahmed yelled indignantly.

When they finally reached the top, Ahmed collapsed to the grass, panting, and covered his eyes.

"It's a girl," Ahmed explained. "She's cute and stuff. She's got history with Ryann, but that's not—"

Blake cut Ahmed off. "So what, who cares?"

"I do," Ryann said firmly. She slung her bookbag to the ground and lay down between Shannon and James. "She's a celebrity. Well, kind of . . . Do any of you remember that project I did for Science Fair last year?"

"No," Shannon, Tomas, and Blake all said in unison.

Ryann scowled. "Okay. Twenty years ago, after NASA was absorbed into the US military, a bunch of private space exploration companies got a ton of investments in, because a lot of people disapproved of the militarization of a public good like space exploration, which made space privatization seem a lot less sinister in comparison. Anyway, there was this company called SCOUT that was super focused on extended missions. They used their investment to gather a bunch of people to send off to the edge of space—"

"Why?" Blake interrupted.

Ryann shrugged. "It was a combination science and art thing. They wanted to have human beings experience the actual journey outside of our solar system. Kind of like the Golden Record, but instead of being there for observation, they're supposed to send back their feelings about the experiences they'll have. Plus, it was a privatized company so their regulations were a bit more flexible. Which leads me to my next point.

"The reason I did my project on SCOUT was because it

was super controversial. Privatized space companies have more flexibility, but they still have to follow general laws. For this mission, SCOUT seemed to be scraping the edge of every limit. Everyone who went had to be at least eighteen so they could personally make the choice to go legally, but young so they'd have around fifty years of mission time. And SCOUT picked only girls because they naturally have better longevity and also did consistently better in psych simulations for long-term travel in tight confines."

"Yikes," Blake said.

"All the candidates were chosen specifically to avoid family attachments," Ryann continued. "But then a journalist uncovered that one of the girls got pregnant and had the kid right before she left. Apparently SCOUT suppressed information about that and waited to deliver the newborn to the family until the candidate left on the mission. Then they covered up their ethical fuckup to avoid bad press, at the expense of a whole family, but news about it wound up getting out anyway. The scandal was so dramatic that a bunch of regulations were passed immediately afterward to stop anything like it from happening again."

"Yiiiiikeessssssss," Blake said, wincing even harder.

"Why isn't any of this more common knowledge?" Shannon asked curiously.

"It happened when we were all maybe one or two years old. It *was* common knowledge and extremely scandalous, but it was a long time ago," Ryann explained. "The only reason I know so much about it is—"

"Because you're a turbo-nerd in love with space-trash. Or at least you used to be," Tomas interrupted. He was texting and barely paying attention.

"Wow." Ahmed turned to scowl at Tomas. "What is wrong with you today?"

"Anyway," Ryann said louder. "The only reason I know about this is because my mom used to be really mad about it and talked about it with her coworkers a lot."

"So what does any of this have to do with anything?" Blake asked.

"*She's* the kid," Ryann said.

Tomas looked up from his phone. "What?"

"The new girl is that kid," Ahmed said. "The one whose teen mom went to *die in space*, Tomas." He slapped Tomas's phone out of his hands and onto the grass. "Did you even listen to any of that? Her name is Alexandria."

Shannon put her chin in her hands contemplatively. "Did she tell you all this herself?"

"No. I . . . haven't spoken to her directly yet. But for obvious reasons, Mrs. Marsh wants me to look after her," Ryann said. She tapped her fingers against the ground anxiously, then turned to Tomas. "Alexandria seems really standoffish in a way that reminded me of you when I first met you, so she probably needs a tougher approach rather than anything straightforward."

"Great," Tomas griped. "More strays."

"You say that like Ryann didn't come to find you, too," Blake said. He picked up Tomas's phone and rubbed it clean with his shirt.

2 HOURS LATER

Ryann walked back to school from the hill to pick up James. He'd left earlier to go to woodshop, one of the after-school electives. James seemed happy to see her and showed her the chair he was building, which was nice. But she kept thinking about the girl from this morning and how rude she was. It was beginning to piss her off all over again.

As they walked over to her bike, James bumped Ryann with his shoulder and raised an eyebrow questioningly.

"It's nothing." Ryann replied.

James scowled and gripped her arm gently, but Ryann shrugged him off and got on her bike.

"Quit it. I mean it," she snapped, revving the engine a bit to drive her point.

But it didn't help. James always knew when she was feeling any type of way.

He climbed onto the bike behind her and put the point of his chin right in her spine. Ryann sucked her teeth in sharp annoyance, but took off anyway.

After a while, James sighed in resignation and laid his head flat against her back. Ryann felt bad for snapping at him.

"I have to pick up some groceries, Birdie," she said gently, using his nickname from when they were little. "Can you carry them?"

He nodded into her jacket. She swerved past the exit home and headed to the store.

30 MINUTES

Ryann didn't like shopping in this town, but she didn't have many other options. Everyone always stared at her and James like they shouldn't be in there. But it had everything they needed, and the pharmacist was nice enough to remember James's name. Even though the prices were a bit higher than in the town they were from, the quality was always better so it was worth it.

Ryann pushed the cart down the cereal aisle and handed a box of Cheerios to James, who had wedged himself in the part of the cart where food usually goes.

"We getting eggs this week?"

James shook his head.

"Do you even like eggs anymore?" Ryann asked.

James scowled and pointed to the next aisle over. Ryann smiled fondly.

"Fine. No eggs this week. But you need prot—"

"We have two more days before the movers send our stuff over?!" someone shouted.

Ryann looked up.

At the end of the aisle was the girl, Alexandria. She was shopping with a stern-looking older blond man, who was clearly ignoring her.

James twisted around to see what Ryann was staring at, then looked up at her in concern.

"It's already been three weeks!" Alexandria continued. "I don't know why—"

Alexandria gazed up the aisle to find the Bird siblings gawking at her. She stopped short, staring back.

Ryann schooled her face into a mask and studied Alexandria.

She was shorter than Ryann had thought from seeing her sitting down this morning. Her hair had been dyed platinum, but she hadn't kept up with it, so dark roots were starting to show. She was one of those people with red splotchy faces who always look like they are about to cry. But her eyes were dark and angry.

Ryann itched to fill the awkward silence with something, but nothing seemed to be right. Instead she looked down at James, gripped the cart railing so tight her knuckles turned white, and pushed the cart down a different aisle.

4 HOURS

Later that night, Ryann lay in her bed. She curled her arm around Charlie and breathed.

The moon washed her room out in light blue, and it was hard to sleep when the sky was so bright. She'd broken her blinds a couple months ago and kept forgetting to get new ones, so James had tacked up one of his extra sheets. But it wasn't completely opaque.

She was so exhausted these days that it was beginning to affect her mood. It was easier now than when Charlie had first arrived a year ago, since he was old enough to sleep through the night these days. But it was still ten times harder to get enough rest than it was before any of this happened.

She pulled out her phone and texted Ahmed.

Ryann: You awake?

Ahmed texted back immediately.

Ahmed: Yes. My parents have friends over and they're being loud as fuck. It's like 1am please come here and kill us all so I can finally find rest in death

Ryann snorted. Drama Queen.

Ryann: That's too much effort. Have you tried asking them to settle down?

Ahmed: Have . . . you met . . . my family . . .

Then a few seconds later:

> **Ahmed:** I'm considering going to sleep in the woods.
>
> **Ryann:** You could always come up here?
>
> **Ahmed:** Too far. Too lazy. I'll just lie here and struggle.

I'll see you tomorrow

THE NEXT DAY

This time, Ryann got to class early. She put her boots up on the desk and motioned for Ahmed to come sit next to her. Ahmed usually sat near the front, but he raised an eyebrow in curiosity and shuffled his supplies to Ryann's right side.

Ryann tapped her pencil on the desk. "I ran into Alexandria in the store yesterday. She reminds me of Blake."

Ahmed snorted. "Blake's an asshole."

"Yeah, but like . . . an asshole in a lonely, isolated, lashing-out way," Ryann said. "She was yelling at her dad in public, which was kind of wild. I feel bad for her."

Ahmed tilted his head back and stared at the ceiling for a solid two minutes, then sighed deeply. "You're not going to feel satisfied until you try to be her friend for real. Like . . . I know Mrs. Marsh asked you to do this, but I *know* you," he said resignedly. "Because that's what you do. Literally compulsively rescuing people from themselves like it's a part-time job or whatever. Just . . . go and try so we can either add her to our group or she can yell at you like she's already yelled at like five other people."

Ryann crossed her arms. "Fine. I will."

3 CLASS PERIODS

The lunchroom was largely segregated by grade and then again by social class. No one was allowed to leave the building for any reason, so it was always packed.

Ryann and her friends usually sat at the back near some of the baseball players. On their other side was the pom-squad. Shannon Greenly from the squad, who was entirely too popular to be hanging out with them in the first place, had moved to the back to sit with Ryann. The entire squad eventually followed and they never left.

Today, however, Ryann opted to seek out Alexandria, who was—predictably—sitting alone. She was wearing a jean jacket and holding her fork in a fist as she scraped at the dry chicken nuggets they were serving today. She looked angry and disgusted. Ryann walked past Tomas, Blake, and Ahmed, who watched her curiously.

Ryann slid her tray onto Alexandria's table and sat down. Ahmed, watching from across the room, silently shook his head.

Alexandria looked up instantly and narrowed her eyes at Ryann.

"Why are you here?" she demanded.

"Why are you alone?" Ryann asked back, popping a french fry into her mouth.

"Why are *you*?" she shot back.

"I'm not." Ryann smiled. "I'm Ryann, we have history together. We don't get new people in this town often, so I'm curious. What's your name?"

Alexandria's mouth pressed into a thin angry line. Then she wordlessly got up, scraped all her food into the trash, and walked out of the lunchroom, leaving Ryann sitting alone.

"YIKES," Tomas yelled from across the room.

Ryann got up, grabbed her tray, and walked to where she usually sat. Shannon patted her hand sympathetically.

"It was a nice try," she said, then turned back to continue her conversation. "Anyway, Samantha's boyfriend's cousin invited Morgan and me to a party tonight. But Jenny's going to be there and I totally hate her because last year she wore the same dress as me to homecoming and she knew I was going to buy that one because I texted her about it beforehand, but she still bought the same one anyway."

"That bitch," Ryann replied. She tossed a french fry into her mouth and gazed at the empty table where Alexandria had been sitting.

"I know." Shannon rolled her eyes. "So anyway, Jenny's boyfriend, Chad, is a huge dick who always gets drunk and tries to fight people, which is totally gross because he's in college. And I don't know whether I want to go tonight and I don't have a ride."

"Eh. You should make an appearance at least," Ryann said after some thought. "Keep your name in other people's mouths. I'll take care of it." She nudged Ahmed with the toe of her boot. "Greenly needs a ride; you wanna party tonight?"

"With who?" Ahmed asked, not looking up from the game of cards he, Blake, and Tomas were playing.

"Prep kids from uptown. Shit music, probably, but they might have free food."

"I'm always a slut for free food," Ahmed said, putting a card down. "What time?"

Ryann looked over to Shannon, who shrugged.

"Pick her up at nine," Ryann said.

AT THE END OF THE DAY

Charlie wouldn't stop fussing. The instant Ryann had pulled him from Ms. Worthing's arms, he'd begun to cry and hadn't stopped after more than an hour.

Ryann jiggled the baby in one arm as she pulled clean clothes off the clothesline in the back, rocked him while she Febrezed her leather jacket, sang to him a bit while she tidied up her room. But nothing seemed to work. Eventually James smacked at Ryann's arms in aggravation, scooped Charlie up, and took him into his room to give him a bottle.

Ryann used the rare moment of freedom to throw on some clean black jeans and a white T-shirt. She put a pot on the stove and put some water on to boil. She took out some macaroni, tomato paste, garlic powder, and cheese, and left them on the counter with some hastily written instructions for James.

Then she tossed on her jacket and knocked on the wall leading to James's room. "Can I come in?"

James knocked back twice, so she opened the door.

"You coming tonight?" Ryann asked, leaning against the door frame.

James shook his head and nodded at Charlie, who had finally dropped off to sleep in his arms.

Ryann watched them for a bit.

"You're better with him than I am," she said quietly.

James shrugged, pulled out his phone, and typed into the notes section: *He's my kid, that's a good thing. Plus, not all girls are domestic. You don't have to be the best at everything.*

Ryann snorted and shrugged. "Yeah whatever."

James raised an eyebrow and continued typing: *Don't get into any fights*

1 HOUR

An hour later, Ryann punched—Chad? Chuck? He was Jenny's boyfriend, whatever his name was—in the throat.

Jenny's boyfriend launched himself across the beer pong table, but Ryann sidestepped him and he fell drunkenly, skidding across the floor. Before he could get up, Ryann sat on his chest, pinning an arm beneath each leg and slapping Chuck? Chad? across the face a couple times with her open palm.

A few people laughed, which made the man even angrier.

"Someone get this trailer trash off me, or I'm calling the cops!" he screamed.

"What the fuck did you just say?!" Ryann leaned in close, daring him to repeat it.

Jenny's boyfriend spat into her face.

Ryann snatched a beer bottle off the ground and smashed the bottom off against the wall, but Ahmed grabbed her arm.

"No, Ryann, no. It's not worth it. Let's just go," Ahmed pleaded.

Ryann dropped the bottle, curled her hand into a fist, and went to punch the guy again, but stopped short.

Jenny's boyfriend flinched.

"You're a coward and you're way too old to be here, you

pompous piece of shit." She got up, rolled her shoulders, and stalked into the kitchen to grab a glass of water. Shannon ran in after her.

"So . . . you guys should probably leave," she said, putting a hand gently on Ryann's arm. "But Jenny's crying now, so I'm having a *great* time. I'll grab a ride home with one of the pom-squad."

"Yeah. *Yeah*. Okay," Ryann agreed, shaking her head, trying to pull herself out of the fog. "We'll take off."

She called out to Tomas and the rest of her friends. Then she paused, leaned down, and patted Shannon on the cheek. "Night, Greenly."

Shannon grinned. "Get home safe!"

30 MINUTES

Ahmed was driving everyone home down a road in one of the nicer parts of town, when Tomas spotted something strange.

Ahead of them, balanced precariously on the edge of the roof of a house, was the new kid from their history class. Alexandria's hair was crisp white in the moonlight, and she wasn't wearing a jacket even though it was getting cold outside.

She was holding her arm up high in the air, and there was something in her hand.

"Pull up next to the house," Ryann said.

Ahmed looked at her warily but did it anyway.

Ryann hopped out of the car and cupped her hand around her mouth.

"Hey, new kid, what the fuck are you doing up there?" she yelled.

The girl turned, looked down to see who was talking to her, then turned completely back around. She didn't respond.

"Yo. Asshole," Blake yelled.

Alexandria didn't even turn around this time.

"Chill out a bit," Ryann hissed.

"Why are you so fucking rude?" she called out instead.

"Who just sits on their roof staring at the sky? It's like

one a.m. We have school tomorrow," Tomas muttered.

"Just let it go." Blake rolled his eyes. "She's a dick, *you're* a dick. Everyone in this school is a dick. Just look her up in the yearbook at the end of the year, or fight her and get it over with."

Ryann glared at Alexandria's back.

"Well now we know she's into astronomy. At least you two have that in common," Tomas said thoughtfully.

"If I don't get a name, I'm making one up," Ryann yelled.

The girl sat so still, but after a second, her head turned—just a little bit—to catch the sound.

Ryann grinned victoriously. *There we are.* She opened the car door and slid inside.

You couldn't nice some people open. Ryann knew that well.

Sometimes the only way to pry your arms away from tightly holding yourself together is when you're given a reason to hold up your fists. Fighting for yourself is another way of loving yourself.

That's the sort of knowledge you have to earn through experience.

It was indelicate, but it was honest. Angry people like Alexandria preferred that kind of honesty. Angry like Tomas had been. Angry like Ryann had been.

NEXT WEEK

They began to bother her.

It was little things at first: bumping her shoulder in the hallway, laughing whenever she said anything in class, mimicking her until her face got red. Eventually, it began to escalate. Tomas knocked her hat off while he was walking by. Ahmed flicked water at the back of her neck for a full class period. Blake filled her locker with bits of paper by painstakingly shoving it all through the tiny slats.

Ryann kept her hands clean.

She never did anything directly, just watched—curious—as Alexandria took it all in silence and rage. Curious, when Alexandria pushed Tomas down the stairs and walked away. When she threw her water bottle at the back of Ahmed's neck when he got up to leave, drenching him as well as he had drenched her and giving him a welt on top of it. When she cleaned up the mess from her locker wordlessly, and then when Blake showed up for school the next day, his entire locker door had been removed from the hinges.

It was like nothing Ryann had ever seen before.

At the moment, Ahmed was casually tossing bits of paper at the back of Alexandria's head—trying to get them to stick in her hair. She was sitting stock-still, only flinching when pieces would tumble free and brush her neck.

Ryann watched dispassionately for a while.

Suddenly, Alexandria gripped her pen like she was ready to stab Ahmed, so Ryann nudged his arm.

"Quit it."

Ahmed sighed loudly and stopped.

After a moment, Alexandria reached up, gently brushed the paper out of her hair and onto the ground, rearranged her pen in her hands, and then continued writing.

Mrs. Marsh caught Ryann's eye. She looked worried. She didn't need to be.

5 HOURS

Mrs. Marsh kept Ryann waiting as she tidied up the room.

"Do you need any help with that?" Ryann asked after a while.

"Do you mind erasing the board and wiping down the whiteboard?" Mrs. Marsh picked up the broom and began sweeping.

Ryann sighed and grabbed the eraser.

"So how are things going with Alexandria?" Mrs. Marsh asked warily. "She seems . . ."

"Angrier?" Ryann replied. "Yeah. You should have seen Tomas though, that whole situation was *much* worse."

"I'm sure."

"No, really," Ryann said as she scrubbed. "He's the only person who's successfully punched me in the face." Ryann added under her breath, "Nearly knocked me the fuck out."

Mrs. Marsh looked shocked. "Did he get suspended?!"

"It wasn't on school grounds, so no. And he did it because I kidnapped him and he woke up in rehab, so . . ."

"Ah."

"Blake was much simpler," Ryann said. "At least no one got arrested."

Mrs. Marsh dumped the dustpan in the trash and stuck

the broom back into the corner. "I don't mean to be frank, but I'm uncomfortable with the way you're handling this. Why do you think this will work? And she seems like she's not reacting well. If you don't get a handle on this, we'll terminate this arrangement and we'll have to have a discussion with the principal about how to resolve any damages."

Ryann shrugged. "It will work itself out, I promise. Besides, my mom used to say that if something that comes hard for others comes easy to you, you should do it for them. Getting people to open up is hard for other people, but it's easy for me."

"You got punched in the face," Mrs. Marsh remarked. "It really doesn't sound easy."

Ryann looked out the window at the other students leaving class. "It is, though. People are easy. We're all made of the same stuff. Even if you arrange it in different ways or make puzzles of it."

Mrs. Marsh grinned. "Do you mean that in a chemistry way or in a psychology way?"

"Both?" Ryann replied seriously. "Maybe the reason the psychology way works is because of the chemistry reason."

Mrs. Marsh bit her lip and drummed her nails on the desk behind her. "Are you in AP psych, chem, or physics?"

Ryann shook her head.

"You should be," Mrs. Marsh said firmly.

"I don't have time for the homework," Ryann replied. She tossed her bookbag over her shoulders.

"But you have time for this?"

Ryann hmmed contemplatively. "I have to go. See you tomorrow."

"It's because this is more important, isn't it?" Mrs. Marsh called.

Ryann closed the door behind her.

BLUR

This part was always difficult for Ryann to remember clearly. There were only bits and pieces that came in fits and starts.

She remembered leaving her bike at school.

She remembered the hazy smoke she shared with Shannon Greenly in the back of Ahmed's car. The kaleidoscope sunshine, and the warmth of James's hand as he dragged it through her hair. She didn't remember who had decided to stop by Blake's and get drinks.

She was just suddenly there and laughing with his friends and someone dropped their keys and that was so funny for some reason.

She had her hand out the car window. Letting her fingers ride the wind's waves.

Then it was night and Tomas wouldn't shut up. And he was doing that stupid dance he did sometimes, while Shannon laughed. She felt grounded by James's soft weight by her side. But it wasn't enough, because Ahmed wanted to do something exciting. He wanted adventure. His black eyes were glittering like beetles.

Ryann slung her arm around Ahmed's neck and joined his howling.

Then the engine rumbled underneath them, screeching

crisp and clear as they whipped down the street. And every-thing was blue and black and blue and black and orange like the streetlights, blurring together until there was a pinprick of white that got closer and closer as Ahmed pressed on the gas, and then Ryann's sneakers hit the pavement outside as they all got out of the car, and then everything went crisp.

8 MINUTES

What happened next was difficult for Ryann to forget.

Rising like a monolith out of the din.

There was the straight back and shittily bleached hair, arm held high, shadow long against the pavement in the light of the moon.

Violent in its relief.

And like Ryann's eyes, had sucked away the senses from her ears. She heard her friends, yelling and laughing like they were at the end of a tunnel, and saw Alexandria sitting on the roof like she was a handbreadth away.

Ryann *knew* Alexandria heard them. She'd flinched the moment they drove up to her house.

Ryann remembered Ahmed yelling something teasing. Nothing mean, but enough to get Alexandria's attention.

Tomas picked up some gravel and tossed it onto the roof from the street. The first rock bounced off the roof and flew back into the garden. The next knocked into an upstairs window, nearly breaking it.

Alexandria turned around, eyes blazing.

"You're pathetic," she shouted.

"That may be true, but what does that make you?" Ryann said back.

Alexandria's face went ashen. She picked up one of the rocks Tomas had successfully landed on the roof and threw it with stunning accuracy.

It launched toward the sidewalk like a comet and struck Ryann on the side of the face, snapping her head back with an audible crack.

2 MINUTES

Ahmed gasped.

"Oh man, she actually hit you!" Blake crowed, laughing nervously.

Ryann clutched the top of her face and sucked air through her teeth to deal with the pain. Then she faced Alexandria, who had gotten to her feet and was staring down at all of them, furious. It was pleasing to feel firsthand that Alexandria was strong. It made Ryann's blood run hot and fast.

"You have good aim." Ryann grinned.

Alexandria's face went soft with confusion.

"What?" she said, and leaned forward.

The roof made a startling noise.

Alexandria scrambled back from the edge instinctively, but overcorrected; the object she was holding flew out of her hand haphazardly. Then like some sort of nightmare, they all watched as she slipped.

Alexandria hit the ground with a smack.

She didn't move or make a sound.

No one breathed.

Then Ahmed immediately turned and ran to his car without looking back. After a couple of horrifying seconds, Blake and Tomas followed.

"Shit! Shit!!" Ryann gasped. She went to run to check if Alexandria was even alive, but James dragged her back with all his might. Somewhere behind him, Shannon was crying.

A light went on in the house, and the curtains were snatched open. Ryann locked eyes with the stern man she'd seen at the grocery store. She wrenched her arm out of James's grip and rushed over to check if Alexandria was all right, but then Alexandria's dad opened the door.

"GET AWAY FROM MY HOUSE!" he roared. "GET AWAY FROM HER!"

His eyes were wide and terrified.

Ryann opened her mouth to say something, but James shoved her into the car.

They sped off into the night.

Ryann and James got home and rushed to Ms. Worthing's and picked up Charlie. Ms. Worthing looked confused when she opened the door.

"Y'all out here, tearin' down the street, white as ghosts!" Ms. Worthing said, pursing her lips suspiciously. "Don't tell me y'all are bringin' trouble round here—"

"We're not," Ryann said quickly. "Thank you for watching Charlie."

As soon as their trailer door closed behind them, James snatched Charlie out of Ryann's arms, took the baby to his room, and slammed the door.

Ryann lay awake for the whole night.

Her heart raced every time she heard sirens.

17 HOURS

Everybody was talking about it the next day at school. No one had the details straight. Some people said Alexandria was pushed. Others said she jumped.

Ryann sat down in the back of her history class, for once not making a racket, and opened her notebook. The seat two desks in front of her was empty.

She hadn't heard anyone mention her name yet, but she was still uneasy.

Ahmed sat down next to her. He looked shaken and exhausted.

"I won't tell," he said. "Blake's and Tomas's parents had them stay home."

Ryann nodded, still staring at the empty chair.

"...?"

Ryann shook her head to clear it, she was sure someone was talking to her.

"...I *said*, how's James?" Ahmed asked again, nudging Ryann's arm.

Ryann shook her head again and rubbed her eyes. "He's not talking to me."

Ahmed chuckled humorlessly. "Not to be a downer, bro. But James doesn't talk to anyone."

Ryann grimaced. There weren't other words to describe what she meant. James had gotten up by himself, fed the baby, and dropped him off. He'd made himself breakfast and left without Ryann. Taking the one bus that went all the way out to where they lived, rather than ride on Ryann's bike with her.

When she got up, the house was cold and empty and there was a note on the table that just said, *Fix it.*

When she saw him in the hallway at school, he'd turned away from her.

James was excellent at holding grudges. He was stubborn, principled, and virtuous, just like their mom had been.

It hadn't even been a day yet and she already missed him.

And there was the hole where Alexandria should be sitting. And Mrs. Marsh's eyes watching her, worried and dark.

32 MINUTES

Mrs. Marsh kept Ryann waiting in silence while she sat and stared out the window. Ryann hadn't felt this way since her mom was alive and making that same face: tired, disgusted eyes with a tight, angry set to her jaw.

Ryann shifted in her chair anxiously.

"Did you do this?" Mrs. Marsh asked quietly.

"Not on purpose."

"Did you push her?" Mrs. Marsh's eyes were still on the other students walking outside.

Ryann swallowed.

"She fell," Ryann replied quietly.

Finally, Mrs. Marsh turned to look at her. "Do you mean that in a literal way, or are you talking around your actions to avoid responsibility for something that may not have happened if you were not there to guide it?"

Ryann didn't know how to answer that without reinforcing Mrs. Marsh's suspicion, so she sat quietly and waited for the lecture that was undoubtedly about to follow.

"You're smart," Mrs. Marsh said. "But you aren't clever. Not all the time. You're a lot of things, but I never expected that cruel was one of them—"

"I was never intending to be cruel—" Ryann interrupted.

"That may be so," Mrs. Marsh said. "But does Alexandria know that? Does her family know? Do your friends know? Do they respect this part of you?"

Ryann didn't know how to answer any of that.

Mrs. Marsh leaned back in her chair and looked at Ryann for a while. "Figure out what kind of person you want to be. Until you make a decision about the repercussions of your actions, I think you should leave Alexandria alone. She doesn't need this, and neither do you."

7 HOURS

After school, Ryann found herself standing outside of Alexandria's house. It looked so different in the setting sun than it did in the night.

Ryann held her breath. She rang the doorbell. Her hands shook, so she shoved them in her pockets.

She thought for a second about leaving, but the door opened quickly. Standing there, white with fury, was Mr. Macallough. He looked more disheveled than the other times she'd seen him, but up close she realized how incredibly young he was. He couldn't have been older than thirty-five.

"I'm sorry," Ryann blurted. She didn't know what else to say.

Alexandria's father stared at her for a bit, studying her from head to toe.

"Have any of the others come?" he asked, in a deep soft voice.

Ryann reflexively looked behind her at the empty street, then turned back and shrugged.

He nodded sharply and something shuttered closed behind his eyes. "Come in. Please don't touch anything."

Ryann followed him into the house and he shut the door behind her.

4 MINUTES

Her heart beat rapidly as she followed him. He was shorter and thinner than Ryann was, and she'd beaten larger people in fights, so she wasn't afraid of him exactly. But it was still very, very awkward as Alexandria's house opened up before her.

The front hallway was lined with gleaming awards and plaques. The walls were papered with maps of the world. Tiny blinking lights snaked up and down the velvety indigo ceiling. Everything was meticulously organized and very beautiful.

She followed Alexandria's dad into a large kitchen with marble countertops, piled high with cookbooks. Copper pans and dried meats hung from hooks in the ceiling. In the back behind a noticeably small kitchen table, there was what looked like some kind of lab.

Ryann had never seen such an aggressive display of wealth in her life.

She gazed down at her scuffed boots on the immaculate tile floor and felt like less than nothing.

"Sit down," Alexandria's father said. "We are going to have a talk."

Ryann sat at the little wooden table awkwardly.

"Alexandria is in the hospital," he said, folding his hands on the table. "You do understand that you put her in the hospital and you absolutely could have killed her?"

"She fell after throwing something at me," Ryann said. "I didn't intend for her to fall or anything, I just—"

Alexandria's dad cut her off. "What you intended has absolutely no bearing on this situation. She has a broken arm and fractured her skull. If you weren't there, if you hadn't been threatening to her, she wouldn't have responded. You were a catalyst and it happened, and now—"

He pressed his lips together angrily, like Ryann had seen Alexandria do, and then he started over. "I'm assuming you know who we are. You wouldn't have been hounding her otherwise?"

Ryann swallowed hard and nodded.

"Do you work for SCOUT?" he asked softly. "Whatever they are paying you, I'll double it if you quit the job."

"What?"

"Are you media, then?" Alexandria's father was undeterred. He pulled out his checkbook and placed it on the table. "You wouldn't be the first young person they've recruited to trail us, and you won't be the last."

Ryann nearly snorted but stopped herself just in time. Alexandria's dad was serious.

"I'm not sure what you're talking about," she said.

Alexandria's dad clenched his jaw angrily. "Be honest," he said quietly. "At least respect us enough for that."

"I . . . ," Ryann started. "Okay. I'm in Alexandria's history class. Our teacher thought Alexandria might have some problems adjusting—no offense—so she asked me to look after her. Try to get to know her."

Alexandria's dad looked surprised. "Why did she pick you? Pardon me for saying so, but you don't really look like the welcoming type."

Ryann grimaced. "You'd think so, but I'm good at it. People with problems often only open up to other people with problems. If they sent some shiny-faced kid with the welcome wagon, do you genuinely think anyone would take that seriously?"

"You sound like someone speaking from experience." Alexandria's dad folded his arms.

"My best friend has had a lot of therapy. Introspection like that rubs off," Ryann replied.

"I can't afford to take your word on that. I'm going to need a signed note from your teacher about this or I'm going to draw up a restraining order."

"Done," Ryann said quickly. "Two questions. One: Why are you so violently paranoid? And two: Alexandria fell while hitting me in the face with a rock after I'd been assigned to look after her, so clearly I read her wrong and fucked things up. I feel . . . like I'm doing a bad job of all this and I'm not comfortable with that, so I came to ask if there is anything I can do to help out with the situation."

Alexandria's dad thought for a minute, then he sighed. "Alexandria does this . . . thing. She, well . . . she does this thing where she likes to sit on the roof to try to see if she can catch messages on this radio scanner she retrofitted with a recording device from . . . Effie. From her mom. I don't like her up there, for obvious reasons . . . Plus, we aren't able to predict when the messages will get here or if any more are coming at all, which is why . . ." Alexandria's dad cleared his throat. ". . . the vigilance. She hasn't missed a single day of doing it for years."

"Are you asking me to fill in for her?" Ryann asked tentatively.

"No, I'm preparing you for her being angry that you destroyed that for her," Alexandria's dad said curtly. "If it's your job to help her adjust, you should know that this is going to be a problem and you should be thinking about how you're going to deal with it when she gets out of the hospital."

Ryann narrowed her eyes. "Sounds difficult. I'd rather just do it instead. It's easier to explain that I've been keeping her caught up than to defend disrupting her work."

Alexandria's dad studied her again. "Are you sure you don't work for SCOUT?" he asked. "This is your last chance to be honest with me."

"Why do you keep asking me that? No. My mom did work for NASA though, in case that bothers you."

"It doesn't." Alexandria's father stood up. "It's getting late; you should start heading home."

Ryann got up and pulled her bookbag onto her shoulders. She followed Alexandria's dad to the door.

"I'm going to need a letter of permission from your parents for you to be here, a signed letter from your teacher regarding the circumstances of your acquaintance with Alexandria, and I'll be doing a background check on you as well. If you decide to follow through, don't get here later than eight p.m. I'll stay out of your way while you work."

"Cool, cool." Ryann stepped onto the porch. "But you never answered my first question. The one about paranoia."

Alexandria's dad stopped short as he was closing the door. He looked at the ground. "I have seen some things that have made me understand that being careful and paying close attention is incredibly valuable. Hopefully you'll live a life where you don't have to learn what that means."

The door closed and the locks clicked tightly shut.

1 HOUR

Ryann pulled the trailer door gently behind her and shut it with a small click.

James was sitting at the kitchen table. He looked up from his homework, frowned, and started to gather his books to retreat to his room.

"Wait. I have something to tell you." Ryann slumped down into the chair across from him. "I went to Alexandria's house to apologize," she said anxiously.

James stopped packing and stared at her.

"Her dad was really upset, but he seems reasonable and it could definitely have been worse," she continued. "You asked me to fix it. I figured out a way to try."

James sat back down. He looked interested.

"That night when we saw her on the roof, Alexandria was trying to catch messages from space. She does it every night and she hasn't missed a single opportunity for years. And she never knows when they're coming. But because she's in the hospital she can't do it anymore. I didn't know that it was something important. I . . . was clumsy and I need to handle my mistake.

"I need you to ask Ms. Worthing if she can watch Charlie a little more for us. I can rebalance our budget to pay her for the extra time. Ride my bike less and get a bus pass . . ."

Ryann finally looked up at James and was surprised to find he was smiling. It was small, but it was there. He pulled out his phone and typed:

This is a good first step you know.

"He won't let me do it unless our parents write a permission letter," Ryann said quietly. "He wants one from a teacher as well so . . . I need you to help with that, too."

James nodded and flipped his notebook to a fresh sheet of paper to begin writing.

Ryann got up and kissed him gently on the top of his head. "Thank you, Birdie."

THE NEXT DAY

Alexandria's father opened the door. He looked over the two sheets of paper Ryann handed him.

"You passed the background check." He scrutinized James's letters. "From a counselor . . . and this other one must be from your legal guardian?"

"Yes," Ryann lied. Technically *she* was James's legal guardian, but that was honestly too much work to explain.

"Have you eaten yet?" he asked.

Ryann hadn't, but she nodded anyway. She couldn't stomach the idea of eating whatever luxuries they had here while James was stuck eating what they had at home. It wasn't fair.

Alexandria's dad led her through the house and up the back staircase. "This is Alexandria's room. Don't touch anything; she'd probably notice." He pushed the door open, and Ryann held her breath.

Alexandria's room was still like a tomb. It was warm and smelled a bit dusty like old paper. The walls had built-in shelves packed tightly with books. There was a wide skylight with a ladder propped against it. She had many small mobiles of stars, planets, and complex flying crafts that swung gently from the ceiling. And from the small mess of paper and wood on her desk, she'd made them all from scratch.

There was a record player set up in one corner of the room and a violin propped up in the other. Her bed was very small and covered in gears, tools, and what appeared to be a disassembled telescope.

Mr. Macallough propped open the skylight and hooked the ladder out onto the roof. "This is where she claims she gets the best reception. Everything you need should be up there. Best of luck."

He left her standing there looking around curiously and shut the door quietly behind him.

2 MINUTES

It felt creepy to be standing in the room of someone who hated her, so Ryann didn't spend any more time looking around. She swung out onto the roof and climbed up to the flat hollow where she'd seen Alexandria sitting.

There was a notebook with some scribbles and some instructions for a brand-new radio recorder, which were clearly left by Mr. Macallough. But there were also a bunch of Alexandria's things that she'd left behind: some candy, a sweatshirt, a retro handheld gaming system Ryann hadn't seen since elementary school called a Galaxy Switch, and a little telescope.

Ryann turned on the radio recorder and propped it up. It played a steady, soft, low static, but otherwise nothing interesting. She frowned and picked up the notebook and flipped through it, but it was just filled with math and calculations in Alexandria's cramped handwriting.

After an hour, she got hungry enough to eat the candy.

Ryann stared at the sky until she felt her eyes starting to close, but it wasn't even midnight yet, so she pinched herself to keep awake.

When she finally got around to turning on the Galaxy Switch, it just opened to a dark screen with white specks on either side of a plus sign in the middle. She clicked left and right a bit, but only succeeded in pushing the plus sign past more white specks. After a little while of playing, she realized it was a super-old space travel game, but it was very boring. She'd almost rather have nothing.

At midnight, she swung off the roof and back into Alexandria's room.

Ryann let herself out of the house and was walking over to her bike when something glittered in the grass. She stopped and looked over to see plastic pieces left from the first radio recorder Alexandria had dropped. She was standing in the exact spot where Alexandria had fallen. Ryann gritted her teeth, then hopped on her motorcycle and rode off into the night.

1 WEEK

After that first excruciating night, Ryann began bringing things up from Alexandria's room to entertain herself.

She started with some books in Alexandria's library.

She pulled the first one off the shelf so gently that the dust around it was barely disturbed and brought it—burning in the inside of her jacket—to the roof.

She made sure to put them back exactly as she had found them each night. Even if it meant having to search for her page the next time she opened one of them.

Alexandria had a lot of classics: Greek tragedies and comedies, and some science fiction, but nothing too campy. Mostly it was textbooks. She also had a small section of poetry. The books were old and didn't look like they'd ever been opened, which was sad.

When it got too dark to see, Ryann lit up the pages with her cell phone. She could barely hear her own thoughts over the sound of the radio's static, so she read out loud more often than not.

Ryann really liked literature. Much more than any other subject, even if it was one of the only classes she was doing poorly in.

She would have given her left arm to have as many books as Alexandria did.

She told her friends about it later, on the hill.

Ahmed was flabbergasted. "You've been in her house? You talked to her *dad*?!"

"Is he pressing charges?" Tomas asked, with the world-weary tone of someone who is sure they're about to get sued.

"He hasn't mentioned anything about that yet," Ryann said. "He just keeps offering me food and being stoic, and he spends all the time I'm there locked up in his room—thank God. Alexandria isn't dead though, in case any of you were wondering."

"You're going over to her house alone with her dad?!" Ahmed shrieked. "What the fuck, Ryann?"

Ryann cut her eyes in Ahmed's direction, then continued her explanation. "He's tiny; I could crack him like a twig. Also, if I keep doing this, and just, like, going over there and stuff, he might forgive us and save our families a lot of hassle. Because I've been in all your houses and I've been in his, and trust me: None of us can afford to get sued by this family."

Blake began rolling his eyes, but Ryann sucked her teeth and snapped her fingers in his direction. "Even you, Blake. I know your dad buys a new car every year, but they have corporate-space-hush money. So lay the fuck off."

"How long do you have to keep doing it?" Shannon asked.

"Until she gets out of the hospital. Or at least that's what Mr. Macallough implied a week ago." Ryann slung her arm around Shannon's shoulder. "What will you all do without me?"

Shannon laughed. "Die of boredom."

"Worry for hours," Ahmed said, crossing his arms.

"Can we come by and see Charlie while you're not there?" Tomas asked. He was lying on his back, staring up at the sky dreamily. "I love babies. I have, like, sooo many cousins."

"Don't drop him, don't scare him, and ask James," Ryann said.

A WEEK AND 3 DAYS

It was a week and a half before anything happened.

Ryann had the radio on full volume. She was lightly dozing with her leg hanging off the roof. It was fifteen minutes before she was set to leave.

Suddenly the radio crackled a bit. Then some light guitar music began to play.

Ryann jerked awake and stared at the radio for a second. Then she picked it up with shaking hands and pressed record.

She sat there on top of Alexandria's house, with the crisp autumn wind blowing through her hair, just listening. The hair on her neck bristling with animal wonder at this... dainty plinking that had traveled from the edges of the solar system just to reach her.

She clutched the radio tight and gazed up into the endless black.

She felt...

She felt...

Indescribable.

3 MINUTES

Ryann ran down the stairs. Her heart was still pounding.

"Mr. Macallough! I caught something!"

Alexandria's dad met her at the bottom of the stairs, hand outstretched for the radio. He rewound a bit and played back what Ryann had recorded. Mr. Macallough listened very keenly, with a hungry look on his face. And when the sound faded out, he closed his eyes for a moment.

Ryann shifted awkwardly on the stairs. She had been coming here so regularly and had barely spent any time with Mr. Macallough, and she'd kind of forgotten that she was intruding. It was more apparent than ever now. She wished, not for the first time, that none of this had happened.

When Mr. Macallough opened his eyes, they were shiny. "'Gnossienne 1,'" he said almost as if to himself, then he shook his head to clear it. "We're going to take this to Alexandria so you can apologize. Go call your parents and tell them where we're going."

Ryann opened her mouth to explain that she didn't have anyone to call, but Alexandria's father had left the room.

She couldn't say no. Not after all this.

1 HOUR

They rode to the hospital in complete silence.

Ryann clutched the radio tightly in her hands and looked out the window at the trees going by in the dark. She felt like she was floating above her body, looking down at herself in the car.

Her chest got tighter and tighter, and the knot in her throat threatened to choke her.

She didn't want to be here.

When they finally reached the hospital, she followed Alexandria's dad inside in a daze.

Alexandria looked very small buried underneath the hospital blankets. Her arm was bandaged up in a sling, she had bandages on the side of her head, and her face had a large purplish bruise to match the purple under her eyes. She was asleep.

Ryann stared at her, stricken.

Alexandria's dad nudged her shoulder a bit to wake her up. After a few tries, Alexandria's eyes fluttered open, and they were as cold and angry as they always had been.

She looked past her father directly at Ryann, and in that moment, Ryann understood what it meant to be judged and found wanting.

"Why is she here," Alexandria said quietly. And it wasn't a question. "What possible reason could you have dreamed up to convince yourself that it was appropriate to bring Ryann Bird . . . *here*."

She glanced up at her father, then turned back to Ryann, and it was terrible, like looking into the sun.

Ryann tossed the radio onto Alexandria's gurney and fled.

It was almost three a.m. when she got home. After walking ten miles, there was no way she was going to school tomorrow.

She dropped her bag onto the kitchen table and changed into some sweatpants and an old T-shirt. Then she picked Charlie up out of his crib and held him close for a bit, until the tightness in her throat and the burning behind her eyes simmered into nothing.

She was so glad the baby was beginning to sleep through the night. She would not have been able to deal with the screaming.

Ryann carried Charlie into James's room and then prodded her brother until he woke up with a grumble and rolled over. He glared at her in sleepy confusion.

"I had a bad night. I'm calling us both in sick, so you can sleep in," she whispered.

Ryann curled an arm around Charlie and shuffled closer until her and James's knees brushed. Her brother reached over and patted his hand across her cheek to check if she was crying. Then, satisfied that she was not, he settled his fingers in her hair.

"I have never felt this small before," Ryann said quietly.

James hummed gently. She knew he didn't think she was small. In this little room, she was all they had.

Ryann closed her eyes. It was still dark out, but the birds outside filled their trailer with song.

THE NEXT MORNING

She woke up to the smell of eggs and Charlie's happy gur-gling. Charlie patted the side of Ryann's head with his fat hands and screamed.

Ryann wiped the drool off her shoulder onto James's sheets and grimaced. She scooped the baby up, tossing him in the air and catching him.

"Who's sweet in the morning? You are! Yes, you are."

Charlie screamed back in agreement.

"Sweet and loud. And hungry, probably."

Ryann carried him into the kitchen where James was cooking and plopped him into his seat.

"We are doing a family thing today because we don't usu-ally," Ryann announced. "All in favor, say, 'Aye!' AYE!"

Charlie shrieked, just because Ryann yelled.

James waved his spatula in a jubilant little motion to show that he agreed.

"Good." Ryann grinned as her brother placed a plate of scrambled eggs in front of her. "We. Are going. To the beach."

30 MINUTES

James wrapped Charlie close to his chest with a long scarf and buttoned his coat over Charlie, snug and tight.

Ryann plunked the helmet they rarely used onto James's head and they roared off toward the highway.

When they pulled up to the rocks by the shore, James hopped off quickly and went to go sit by the waves. Just close enough that they just barely touched the toe of his boot.

Ryann eventually settled down beside him.

It was too cold to do anything but sit. The sand was dense and crunchy and the air tasted like salt, but it was soft and clean.

James curled up close and wrapped his arms around his baby like he had a stomachache. Charlie's wide brown eyes blinked at Ryann curiously through the gap.

"Do you think he would've liked Mom and Dad as parents better than us?" Ryann asked quietly.

James shrugged.

Ryann watched her little brother as he nuzzled the top of Charlie's head with his nose, and she wished, with every bit of herself, that she could hear his voice again.

"I miss them, Birdie," she whispered. Barely audible over the crashing surf. "You're a good dad anyway though."

James reached over and pulled at her black tangled hair until she curled up with her head on his knee. Then he fumbled his phone out of his pocket and took a picture.

"Making family albums again?" Ryann murmured.

James smirked and stroked her cheek.

4 HOURS

Tomas and Blake were sitting on their steps when the Birds got back to the trailer park.

"Flock of three!" Blake hooted, stubbing out his cigarette on the concrete.

Tomas kissed James on the cheek, then stretched out his arms and made grabby motions with his hands until Charlie was deposited in his grasp. "Yuss."

Charlie patted at Tomas's face and grabbed at his bright red Mohawk curiously.

"Hands! Keep his hands clean," Ryann warned as she tucked her bike away on the side of the trailer.

"Of course, we'll keep his hands clean, won't we? Won't we, Charlie?" Tomas cooed.

Ryann rolled her eyes.

Tomas and Ryann went to the back of the trailer, while Blake followed James inside. Ryann started working on a bonfire.

Tomas lay down in the leaves with Charlie on his chest. He took a package of wet wipes out of his jacket and cleaned Charlie's hands dutifully.

"So, James texted us all that you got a transmission," Tomas said faux casually.

Ryann cut her eyes to Tomas quickly, but said nothing.

"You're spending a lot of time out there, at her house," Tomas remarked.

Ryann pulled out her lighter, lit a dry twig, and tossed it onto the pile of wood. She didn't respond as she settled back on the heels of her boots and gazed into the flames.

"She's resilient," Tomas continued after a pause. "I like that."

"You would," Ryann said, grinning.

Tomas put a hand down Charlie's back and frowned.

"I don't have problems with new blood, and I'm sure the space stuff with Alexandria is interesting, I just don't know if it's a good focus point. You haven't been around a lot lately, and things are changing up underneath you. Ahmed's been spending *a lot* of time with Greenly while you've been otherwise occupied. You'll notice that neither of them are here." Tomas's eyes glittered in the firelight. "Get a handle on your empire, Constantine."

Blake and James came back with supplies for s'mores, and the rest of the night went on without a hitch, but Ryann thought about what Tomas had said for hours.

3 WEEKS

Ryann let herself into their house this time. Alexandria's dad wasn't in the kitchen.

He was sitting, reading, in the living room, and he was significantly more put together than Ryann had seen him since Alexandria's fall. It was unusual, and the house felt like it had a different energy. Even though, other than Alexandria's dad being in the living room, nothing seemed to be out of place.

"Hi," she said nervously.

He looked up from his book. "There is some food in the kitchen if you want it," he said, then he went back to reading.

Ryann glanced into the kitchen as she walked past on her way to the stairs.

43 SECONDS

Of all the things Ryann Bird had expected to find in Alexandria's room, Alexandria herself was strangely not one of them. So when she opened the door to find Alexandria struggling to get into the skylight, trying to reconcile her broken arm with the height of the windowsill, Ryann just . . . stared for a bit.

"Were you born in a barn? Is knocking a foreign concept for you?" Alexandria said sharply. The bandages on her head were gone and the bruises had faded. Her hair was still shorter in one place where they must have shaved it down to put in stitches. Ryann stared at Alexandria dumbly for longer than was appropriate before snapping out of it and walking into the room.

"You shouldn't be doing that," Ryann said, watching Alexandria try a new angle to wedge herself up. "You're going to get hurt again."

"First of all, I didn't 'get hurt.' *You* startled me. And second of all, I can do this by myself. You can leave." Alexandria tried to jump a bit, but without being able to reach, she was too short to pull herself up.

Ryann looked back down the stairs. If Mr. Macallough hadn't wanted her here to do this, he would have told her so in the living room.

"Okay, get out of the way. I'll go out and pull you up." Ryann shouldered Alexandria aside and pulled herself through the skylight. Then she lay down and put her arms through the opening. It was a moment before Alexandria grabbed on to them; which was ridiculous because Ryann knew she was standing right there.

She hefted the other girl up until they were both on the roof. Alexandria quickly snatched herself out of Ryann's grip.

She crawled over to the spot where Ryann had been sitting for almost two months and took stock of it.

"So you've been snooping in my room and ate all my candy. That sounds fair," she said sarcastically. "Anything else?"

"I played with your Galaxy Switch." Ryann sprawled out and crossed her arms behind her head.

"If by 'played' you mean 'fucked my charting up, displaced my ship, and put me eight weeks of work behind.'" She brushed the candy wrappers and paper cranes Ryann had made out of the way with a sneer of disgust. Then Alexandria took out her notebook and started writing furiously. "Just. Don't touch anything else. And be quiet," Alexandria snapped.

3 HOURS

They spent the night in complete silence.

Ryann dozed off a bit. Every time she woke up, she had the feeling she was being watched, but by the time she opened her eyes or turned around, Alexandria was busy writing.

At midnight, Ryann got up and stretched. "I'm going home and that means you need to get down. Unless you want to stay up here all night."

"I'm staying until one," Alexandria said. "Whether you come or go is of no consequence to me."

"Oh my God, fine!" Ryann snarled. She slumped back down onto the roof and lay there for another hour.

At exactly one a.m., Alexandria folded up her notebook and gathered all the loose paper Ryann had left on the roof and put it all in the pocket of her sweatshirt.

Ryann shook her head to wake herself up a bit, climbed down the roof, and swung inside through the skylight. She stuck the front half of her body back out and sleepily held up her arms to catch Alexandria and guide her down safely back to her bedroom floor.

Alexandria tugged herself free of Ryann's grip as soon

as her shoes hit the ground, and she was giving Ryann a strange and not at all friendly look. But Ryann was too exhausted to care.

"Mmkay. G'night," Ryann slurred. She tugged her book-bag onto her back and trudged out of Alexandria's room.

TUESDAY MORNING

Ryann was always late, so she didn't bother to hurry. Plus, she'd been sleeping in through history for the past eight weeks because of the stargazing, and she was pretty sure if she didn't show up eventually, they'd start sending letters home or notify the truancy police.

She slammed the door open and walked in, passing right in front of Mrs. Marsh and obscuring the light of the projector—plunging the classroom into darkness.

"Thank you for gracing us with your presence, Ms. Bird," Mrs. Marsh drawled.

Ryann shrugged and trudged to the back of the room.

"Bird," Shannon Greenly said demurely.

Ryann scrunched her nose up and grinned.

She walked past Alexandria's desk. They locked eyes for a second, but Alexandria looked away quickly and went back to writing her notes.

Ryann dropped her bookbag onto the floor and settled down next to Ahmed.

"Where the fuck have you been?" Ahmed sneered.

"You know where I've been. I've been busy," Ryann said. "Sounds like you've been busy, too."

Ahmed looked angry, but also embarrassed.

"You have my blessing on it, by the way," Ryann said quietly, flicking her eyes over to Shannon. "Congratulations."

"I don't know what you're talking about," Ahmed said and slumped lower in his seat.

Ryann grinned and slung an arm around Ahmed's shoulder. Ahmed tried to wriggle away, but Ryann was bigger. She leaned all her weight into it. Some of the other students turned around to watch.

Eventually Ahmed's chair couldn't take it, and they both fell to the floor with a loud bang and a shriek. Ahmed's pencil case flew off his desk in the scuffle and showered Jasmine and Privati in writing utensils.

Ryann kissed Ahmed smack on the cheek loudly. Ahmed hissed in disgust and wiped his face.

"I missed you, too."

6 CLASS PERIODS

For the first time in more than two months, Ryann didn't walk to Alexandria's house after school. She went to detention.

Ahmed sat next to her, arms crossed.

"So. Greenly." Ryann put her boots on the desk.

"Your feet belong on the floor," the detention monitor snapped.

Ryann crinkled her eyebrows disrespectfully, then turned back to Ahmed. "Anyway. How did that start?"

"Well. While you were at Alexandria's house making goo-goo eyes at her dad, Shannon invited us out to a party and we started talking."

Ryann whipped her feet off the desk and pressed a hand to the center of her chest and gazed at Ahmed beseechingly. "I am so offended."

Ahmed cracked a small smile.

"But, seriously though." Ryann grinned back, running a hand through her messy hair. "I'm not hanging around there to be with Mr. Macallough. It's not like that. He barely speaks to me."

Ahmed snorted. "It would be weird and problematic if he did."

"He does try to feed me though," Ryann said contemplatively.

"So do I, if you're around," Ahmed shot back.

"Alexandria's room is cool. Lots of books. It's weird though. I've spent so much time in her room touching her stuff that it almost feels like we know each other," Ryann admitted. "She's a decent kid. Really smart."

"Oh no. Not this again," Ahmed said. He scooted his desk around so he was facing Ryann completely. So that his accusatory glare would have full effect. "Don't drag her into our group. Just do what Mrs. Marsh asked, be happy we aren't being brought up on charges, and let it go. I'm still recovering from the last time you did this."

Ryann scowled, offended this time. "I know you didn't like Tomas, but you like him now! Everyone I add to our friend group is good!"

"Tomas is a dick. He was a dick; he is a dick. He will always. Be. A dickhead." Ahmed punctuated his sentences with sharp jabs to Ryann's shoulder. "I'm not spending my last year here hanging out with another social charity case!"

"Come on, Ahmed."

Ahmed scowled. "If you ditch with me, I'll consider it."

Ryann flicked her gaze to the door, then slid her eyes over to the detention monitor.

Without any warning, she bolted, flinging open the door and sprinting outside. She looked over her shoulder, and, like always, Ahmed was grinning and running behind her.

28 MINUTES

Ahmed parked his car out by the beach.

He rolled himself some spliff and smoked until the windows were opaque and their eyes burned.

Ryann leaned her head back on the headrest.

She never smoked, but sometimes she did this: just leaned back and let Ahmed smoke for her.

"You know what? Do what you want, man," Ahmed said suddenly.

Ryann grinned. She could almost hear Ahmed rolling his eyes.

"I know you're probably smiling. All goofy and dumb." Ahmed waved the smoke away so he could catch a glimpse of Ryann's face. "Yeah. There it is. You're such a punk. Way too nice for me to have to pull your problematic ass off people once a month." Ahmed coughed and smacked Ryann on the back of the head. "Just get it over with. And don't get all sad if she doesn't want to be friends with you."

Ryann just closed her eyes and breathed deep.

They stayed out by the shore until dark.

3 HOURS

Alexandria crinkled her nose the instant Ryann walked into her room.

"I'm sorry," Ryann tried preemptively.

"I'm *NOT* going up there with you while you smell like that," Alexandria spat.

"Fine. Whatever. It's not like I haven't been alone up there for the past two months or anything." Ryann swung herself up through the skylight and sat on the edge with her legs dangling into Alexandria's room.

"Wow. That is actually worse than if you were completely inside my room."

"I'm trying, okay?" Ryann frowned. "I get being rude is your thing, but does it have to be constant?"

"I wonder why? I wonder why it could be that I'm rude to you," Alexandria said sarcastically. "Perhaps it could be because your friends keep slamming me into whatever object is both reasonably hard and conveniently near. Or because you and your horrible friends got to watch me break my arm and fracture my skull, and laughed when I fell off a building. Or because you hate me, but somehow made friends with my dad, so I must see you at home *and* at school. Or it could be because you're making my room reek of weed. I mean, we have a veritable buffet of options. Pick whichever one you like."

"I'm sorry."

"What?"

Ryann hopped back down into Alexandria's room, landing right in front of her. Alexandria flinched, but then looked even *angrier*, so Ryann backed up a bit.

"Look." Ryann sighed. "I'm sorry. Okay? I didn't mean for that to happen. I know that's not an excuse and it doesn't make your arm less broken, but there it is. Also, no one laughed when you fell. It wasn't funny, it was scary."

Alexandria didn't say anything, so Ryann plodded on. "Also, I'll get Blake, Tomas, and Ahmed off your back. I don't actually control them. Plus, they've definitely stopped since you went to the hospital . . . I can get them to apologize, but I can't go back in time and stop them. I also can't do anything about the weed. That's pretty much gotta stay." She chuffed humorlessly and brushed a hand through her tangled hair. "But I've been doing this for a while. More than a while. I wouldn't be here if I didn't think this was important. And I don't hate you. I just . . . Sometimes I have a temper about certain topics. It's not your fault. I swear, I'm working on it."

"Pencils. Are pencils one of those topics?" Alexandria asked.

Ryann frowned.

"When you can't afford things as easily, yeah. I guess they are." She pushed past Alexandria and lifted herself back up onto the roof.

5 HOURS

When Ryann finally swung back down, Alexandria was crouching by her bookcase. She looked over her shoulder quickly, then ran her fingers along the edge of a shelf.

"You have sticky fingers," she said quietly.

Ryann picked up her bookbag and put it on. She was exhausted. She didn't have time for this.

"You can . . . borrow the books if you want," Alexandria said. "Whenever you like."

2 DAYS

Alexandria shut her notebook and stared up at the sky. Then she pulled out her Galaxy Switch thing.

Ryann looked up from *The Iliad*, curious. "So what is that, anyway?"

"It's a game I designed that simulates the calculated trajectory of my mom's ship."

Ryann sat up. "You're using *that* to simulate a spaceship??"

"That's what I just said, yes," Alexandria replied.

"That's so cool! Wow. Can I—"

Alexandria swung around so her cast was blocking Ryann from seeing over her shoulder. "For Christ's sake, you touch literally everything of mine all the time. It just looks like darkness and dots. Plus, I just finished fixing my calculations from after you wandered my ship all over the outer reaches of the solar system while I was lying helplessly in bed."

Ryann scowled. "Oh my God, you're so mean," she muttered.

Alexandria sighed very loudly. "Will you stop whining if I play some music?"

Ryann smirked and lay back, propping *The Iliad* on her chest and looking up at the stars. "I'll consider it."

1 HOUR AND 28 MINUTES

Between the light of her phone and the light of Alexandria's Galaxy Switch, the stars didn't look as bright.

Despite the music, the quiet was as quiet as it always was. And the space between them was as vast as it always was.

And Alexandria sat no less straight and stiff than when Ryann first met her.

But things were feeling a little different.

Ryann remembered when she'd first met Blake. When Blake had grinned up at her with blood between his teeth, as Ryann looked down at him with blood between her knuckles, and he said—in that knowing way that he said *everything*: "I'm not who you want to be hitting, am I?"

When she'd first met Tomas, slumped inside the bathroom. Half gone already. How she'd shoved her fingers down that kid's throat and saved his life.

When she'd first met Ahmed.

And, somehow, the curve of Alexandria's spine looked less aggressive and more nervous.

"Quit staring at me," Alexandria said.

"What else is there to look at?"

"Literally everything."

Ryann closed her eyes.

2 HOURS AND 3 SECONDS

Ryann put Alexandria gently back down onto the floor, and, like always, Alexandria snatched herself hurriedly out of Ryann's grip. She tossed her notebook onto her desk and glanced over her shoulder at Ryann suspiciously.

"So when did you start doing this?" Ryann asked, leaning in closer.

"My dad did it for a while, and then I picked it up when I was maybe in middle school. Why?"

Ryann shrugged. "You must have like hundreds of transmissions or something by now."

Suddenly Alexandria looked really busy shifting things around on her desk. "We only have about ten," she said quietly.

"That's so weird. She's only sent ten in all this—"

"No. She hasn't only sent ten; we just can't . . . it's hard for . . . I don't . . ." Alexandria's face was red and splotchy as she searched for the right words. Ryann watched curiously. She'd never seen Alexandria lose her composure before, and it was fascinating—if not a little awkward.

"You know what, you don't have to tell me right now," Ryann said. "But, if you're interested, me and my friends are having lunch on the hill tomorrow. You can come if you want to."

Alexandria scowled, finding quick comfort in anger. "Why would I do that?" she spat.

Ryann shrugged again and headed downstairs. "It's better than eating alone."

1 WEEK

Ryann lay on her back, chewing on a piece of grass. Ahmed and Shannon sat behind her, chatting quietly to each other and sitting very close. Every so often Shannon would twirl her finger in Ryann's hair. Ahmed was doing that dumb leg jiggle thing he did when he got nervous. He was hitting Ryann in the shoulder at three hundred beats per minute.

Ryann closed her eyes and tried to will some confidence into Ahmed, because if the jiggling didn't stop this instant—

James touched Ryann's arm gently and she opened her eyes.

"You have a new record. It took me at least three months to trudge up here," Tomas murmured contemplatively.

Ryann remembered what she had said last night and sat up quick as a shot.

Alexandria was heading up the hill. Jaw clenched. Knuckles white. She looked murderous.

Ryann smiled and waved.

James seemed confused and suspicious. He pinched Ryann and nodded in Alexandria's direction. Ryann shrugged his hand off.

"Ahmed. Promise me you'll be nice," Ryann hissed.

"I promise. Jeez," Ahmed griped.

Shannon gazed at Alexandria with placid curiosity as

she trudged up to them. Before Ryann could say anything or introduce anyone, Tomas stood up and stuck out his hand. "I'm sorry for pulling on your hair," he said.

"No, he's not," Blake snorted in the background.

"Blake is an asshole. We're all assholes. I'm sorry about that, too." Tomas shrugged and put his hand back into his sweatshirt pocket when it was clear Alexandria wasn't going to shake it anytime soon.

"So. Anyway," Ryann said slowly, narrowing her eyes at Tomas. "This . . . is Alexandria. She's probably the smartest person I've ever met. She doesn't have anyone here yet, so until she does, we're all she's got."

Alexandria's face went from soft surprise right back into a scowl at that last part. But Ryann still patted a spot in the grass next to her. Eventually Alexandria settled down and opened her lunch box.

"This is Ahmed, Blake, Tomas, Shannon Greenly—who you probably know already," Ryann continued, pointing at everyone. And this . . . is my brother, James."

James gazed at Alexandria keenly. Alexandria stared back.

When she eventually looked away, James lifted his phone and took a picture.

9 HOURS

When Ryann rang Alexandria's doorbell, Mr. Macallough opened the door and looked at her sternly for a minute. Then he held up a key.

"I don't want to have to answer the door every night anymore. It's been more than a month and you haven't stolen anything, so you've earned this. Don't abuse it, or I'll change the locks," he said.

Ryann was shocked. She took the key and zipped it up safely in her bookbag. When she looked back up to stutter a thank-you, Mr. Macallough was gone.

She took the stairs two at a time, knocked quickly at Alexandria's door, and then opened it.

Alexandria was standing in the center of her room, holding a letter tightly. Her face was splotchy and red.

"Your dad gave me a key—"

"Shut up, I'm reading," she hissed.

Ryann scowled and dropped her bookbag loudly on the ground. She leaned against Alexandria's desk and waited.

"Fuck. *Fuck*," Alexandria said.

Ryann raised an eyebrow.

"SCOUT is looking for recruits."

Ryann raised her eyebrow higher.

"They're looking for recruits for the next cohort," Alexandria explained frantically. "They're looking for people to send to space. For girls our age to send to space! Ryann!"

"Okay?" Ryann said.

"OKAY?! ARE YOU KIDDING ME?" Alexandria yelled excitedly. She glanced at the door, then lowered her voice to a tight whisper. "Do you know what this means??"

Ryann walked across the room and opened the skylight. "I doubt you'll be able to travel fast enough to catch up with the last cohort," Ryann said. "And if so, why would you even want to go?"

Alexandria's face closed off so quickly Ryann did a double take. Alexandria tilted her chin up and stared at Ryann dangerously. "What did you say?"

"Why would you want to go?" Ryann repeated. "I mean . . . this is the result of what happened," she said, throwing her arms out in frustration "They're just making more versions of all this. More families who are feeling all this. I thought that was the whole point of why you do . . . what you do?"

Alexandria shook her head. "You don't understand. You never did—I can't believe—" She ran her fingers through her hair agitatedly, then pinned Ryann beneath her gaze again. "Why are you here?" Alexandria demanded lowly.

"Because I—"

"WHY ARE YOU HERE?"

"Because you needed help," Ryann said. "Because I care about all this."

Alexandria closed her eyes and took a deep breath. "Get out of my house."

"What is your fucking problem?"

Alexandria marched across the room, opened the door, and threw Ryann's bookbag into the hallway. "I almost thought—" she started, then paused and shook her head again and pointed to the door. "Get out."

Ryann strode angrily across Alexandria's room and picked up her bag. "You're an asshole," she spat.

Alexandria slammed the door shut.

When Ryann got home, she went immediately to bed. Her heart was still racing.

She genuinely couldn't comprehend the interaction she'd just had.

Who the fuck spends years pining after someone and then blindly just decides they would want to do the same thing to their own family? Alexandria's dad had no one. What would he think if he found out Alexandria was hoping to leave?

And who the fuck does she think she is, pushing Ryann— who was just trying to help—out of her room like that?

The more Ryann thought about it, the angrier she got. She dug in her bookbag for the key Alexandria's dad gave her, intending to chuck it outside somewhere. But when it finally found its way into her hand, she suddenly felt more sad than angry.

Ryann sat on the edge of her bed and held the key in her hand for a while. She turned it over. Mr. Macallough had gotten her name embossed at the top.

She tucked the key in a small pocket for safekeeping and went to sleep.

THE NEXT DAY

Ryann was always late, so she didn't bother to hurry.

She was exhausted and red-eyed. She slammed the door open and walked in, passing right in front of her history teacher and obscuring the light of the projector—plunging the classroom into darkness.

"Late again, Ms. Bird?" Mrs. Marsh drawled.

"Sorry," she mumbled absentmindedly.

"Bird," Shannon Greenly said demurely as she passed her desk.

Ryann didn't seem to hear her.

She walked past Alexandria's desk. Alexandria was staring determinedly out the window. The corners of her mouth were turned sharply down. Ryann's eyes flickered across her face, but even though she knew Alexandria could tell she was being watched, she stubbornly looked even farther away.

Ryann dropped her bookbag on the floor and settled down next to Ahmed.

"Hey, are you okay?" Ahmed asked.

Ryann shook her head. She tore a bit of paper off her notebook and wrote: *I'm sorry.*

She nudged Ahmed. "Hey, can you pass this to Alexandria?"

Ahmed frowned but did as he was asked.

Alexandria stared at the note for almost five minutes solid. Then she crumpled it up and put it in her jacket pocket.

4 HOURS

Mrs. Marsh sat down next to Ryann at Sam Wellington's desk. She waited patiently, grading papers until Ryann spoke first.

"I fucked up and I'm not sure how."

Mrs. Marsh put her pen down and folded her hands. "Did you try apologizing?"

"Saying sorry isn't hard. That was the first thing I did," Ryann said, scowling. "Alexandria is difficult. She's private and hard to read."

"What happened?"

Ryann bit her lip and jiggled her foot anxiously. "Yesterday I went over to her house, and she had a letter that she got from SCOUT. Apparently they're doing another mission, and she was really excited to go for some reason. She started talking about applying, but then she asked me why I wasn't as excited as she was.

"I told her that I didn't understand why she was so excited, because literally everything terrible that's happened to her is directly related to SCOUT. Then she got really quiet and angry and threw me out of her house. Like literally threw my bookbag into the hallway. Like . . . on one hand, I know I probably should have been less frank. But on the other hand,

I didn't say anything that she didn't already know, so—"

Mrs. Marsh pushed the papers she was grading aside. "How do you know how she feels about what happened? Have you talked to her about it?"

"No, but I've read about it, and she spends every night trying to reconnect in some way with her mom, and SCOUT is responsible for that. I don't get why she would be excited to tear her own family even further apart."

Mrs. Marsh smiled. "There it is. You're looking at her situation from your own perspective. You would be severely impacted by the same circumstances, so you're assuming that she has been as well. But family means different things to different people.

"I think you should give Alexandria the opportunity to explain what happened herself. Reading about something isn't the same as living through it. Every story has many sides, depending on where you're standing when it happens."

Ryann leaned back and looked at the ceiling tiles. "I should've known that already."

"You don't have to know everything all the time. It's okay to lose perspective." Mrs. Marsh gathered up her paperwork and put it in her desk. "As long as you try your best—and I feel like you are—I think you'll work this whole thing out."

6 CLASS PERIODS

As soon as the day was over, Ryann sped out of class to the front exit.

She waited until she saw Alexandria's white hair in the crowd and made her way over to her. Alexandria spotted her out of the corner of her eye and started walking faster, to get away. Ryann increased her speed, too, until she was close behind her.

"Alexandria!" She reached out to grab the other girl's arm, but Alexandria ripped it out of her grasp.

"Go away," Alexandria hissed.

"I'm sorry, all right? I overstepped your boundaries and said some things I shouldn't have—" Ryann began, but Alexandria kept walking. People were starting to watch.

Alexandria diverted her path away from the crowd, but kept up her speed. "Stop following me."

"Stop ignoring me!" Ryann shouted.

Alexandria whipped around to face her with the full force of her anger, but whatever she saw on Ryann's face made her falter.

Ryann quickly took advantage of it. "Look," she said, "I get that I shouldn't have said what I did, and I get that the whole SCOUT thing is really important to you—"

"No. You don't," Alexandria spat. "You don't even know anything about it. So don't pretend you do."

Ryann stood her ground. She reached out her hand and, in a very gentle voice, said, "I know. I'm sorry. But I want to know, if you're willing to tell me."

18 MINUTES

Alexandria drove Ryann home with her. The car was silent, and she was a terribly aggressive driver.

Ryann clutched the door handle and kept glancing over nervously. She knew by now that just because Alexandria looked angry enough to tear someone to pieces, it didn't mean she would. But Ryann wasn't about to take chances.

"You can relax; I'm not going to kill us." Alexandria rolled down the window and spat.

"I could, honestly, tell you the same without changing any words," Ryann said. "And it would still be accurate."

Alexandria swerved violently into the parking space in front of her house and jerked on the brake. Then, before Ryann could get out, Alexandria turned to her with stern brown eyes and said, "Why does this mean so much to you?"

Ryann glanced at Alexandria's hands, which were still gripping the steering wheel so hard her knuckles were yellow.

"I know when something is important," Ryann said honestly. "And I know when I'm lucky enough to get an opportunity to be a part of something important. And I think that, whatever you're about to tell me, it's probably both of those things."

An expression flashed across Alexandria's face, but she quickly hid whatever it was and replaced it with a determined scowl. "That's good enough," she said. "Come with me."

7 MINUTES

Alexandria led her inside, but instead of going up to her room, they went downstairs to the basement. Alexandria pulled a string, and all the lights went on.

The entire room was crammed with books and odds and ends. There was a giant globe covered in stars in the middle of the room. The walls were wallpapered with star charts and giant blown-up photographs. There were telescopes that ranged from arm-length to nearly the size of a person. Ryann badly wanted to start exploring, but the moment wasn't right.

Alexandria stopped in front of a letter on the wall. It was framed and spotlighted.

Ryann came up next to her.

"In the late 1970s, NASA sent out a record that was meant to portray the diversity and beauty of all life on Earth, called the 'Golden Record,'" Alexandria explained quietly. "They scoured the planet for meaningful tokens of the accomplishments of humanity: songs, literature, the sounds of birds and animals. Then they sent the record on a spacecraft called *Voyager*, to travel the stars until something—anything—finds meaning in it."

Alexandria folded her arms tight over her chest and turned to Ryann. "This mission . . . it's like being a living

Golden Record. It's not about selfishness or your family or what you feel about anything. It's one of the greatest honors that exists. When my mother got in, more than twenty million people from all over the world had applied."

"Oh," Ryann said softly.

"Having you stand in the middle of my room, and talk about it like it was . . . *a field trip* that I probably shouldn't go on was one of the most disrespectful things I have ever experienced," Alexandria said. "But it was terrible only because I expected you to know that, and when you didn't, it became very clear that we had been doing two very different things for the past few weeks."

Ryann nodded. She didn't know what to say.

"Do you still want to help me with the transmissions?" Alexandria asked. "Do you understand what this is now?"

"Yeah."

"Pinkie promise?" Alexandria said coldly.

Ryann nearly laughed, but she caught herself just in time. Alexandria wasn't at all kidding. She still looked as incandescently furious as she had the day before.

Curious and thankful, Ryann held up her pinkie, and Alexandria locked their fingers together.

3 HOURS AND 57 SECONDS

They were lying directly beneath Canis Major when Ryann turned to Alexandria and said, "I did a project on this last year. When I first saw you, I wasn't able to make the connection and figure out who you were, but by the end of the day I knew the whole story. Even before all of this."

"I know," Alexandria replied.

"How?"

Alexandria turned a page in her notebook and continued writing. "You started looking at me like ... I don't know. I could just tell."

Ryann hmmed.

"I hated it," Alexandria said quietly. "You didn't earn the right to pity me."

"I don't pity you."

Alexandria looked up, startled away from her calculations. She gazed at Ryann in silence.

Ryann looked steadily back. She wasn't a coward. "All I know is from what I read. Everything about what happened to your family was from the perspective of other people. I had no other choice but to take their word for it."

Alexandria closed her notebook and sat up. "You could've asked." She said gently, "I would tell you ... if you asked."

"Eighteen years ago there was a call for volunteers. There was going to be a trip, and they wanted young people—smart, curious young people—to go. It was the chance of a lifetime, but very secret, as all good things are. They wanted ten people to go up into the stars and float away as far as they could go. To see the cosmos with human eyes and to be a living record of the people of Earth, for everyone back home not brave enough to follow.

"They were the first explorers. The first Uninauts."

The wind on the roof blew hard. Alexandria flipped up the collar of her jean jacket and continued. "They ran a lot of tests and searched through hundreds of people, until they settled on a small crew. All of them were seventeen or eighteen years old. Young enough to last a while.

"The first was a girl from the Congo, the brightest in her class. The next three were Russian, engineering whizzes. Very nice, I've been told. There was a young bio-chem major from China, whose whole family attended the launch. An Englishwoman who did independent study in robotics.

"Two Swedes from a biology program, a Mexican heiress who snuck her guitar onto the ship, and an American called

Eferhilde. A nice girl, with a knack for problem-solving. My eyes are her eyes, and my hair is her hair—at least what I can tell from pictures."

Alexandria tapped her fingers on the roof tiles and then looked past Ryann and out into the neighborhood. "She was only seventeen when she left home for training."

"When . . . did she learn about you?" Ryann asked.

Alexandria shrugged. "I'm not sure, but she didn't know she was pregnant when she left for training. Training was like a sleepaway camp and lasted almost a full year. She went, learned about me, had me, and maybe got to be with me for a while before she went to space. My dad said that when a representative from SCOUT arrived on his parents' doorstep, I was at least three or four months old. He won't talk to me much about what happened around then, but he was only eighteen when they dropped me off. He hadn't even graduated high school yet."

"Oh," Ryann said. She thought about James and Charlie.

"He blames SCOUT for it. He didn't have any time to emotionally prepare for any of it. They handled things badly, so he doesn't trust them."

Ryann snorted. "When I came by after you fell, he accused me of working for them and spying on you."

Alexandria pressed her lips together and jiggled her foot. "Strange things have happened to us."

"I'm sorry," Ryann said.

"Don't pity me," Alexandria said.

"I don't," Ryann said. "But I'm sorry anyway."

James was waiting up for her when she got in.

Ryann put a pot on the stove to boil some water and sat down across from him at the kitchen table. "Have you ever had a secret so big that it made you want to yell and punch things?" she asked.

James grinned wryly and nodded over at Charlie's crib.

"Yeah, yeah, I know. I know. Tell me when you're ready." She reached over and knit their fingers together. "I missed you. How is the bike handling? Does it need anything? Do you feel safe getting back and forth to school by yourself?"

James nodded and rolled his eyes, pulling out his phone. *Alexandria?* he typed.

"She's fine."

James raised an eyebrow, but decided not to press her further. Instead, he typed, *Charlie said a word today.*

"Oh my God, seriously? What was it? How come I always miss all the good stuff?"

James shrugged.

"What was it?"

He typed and turned his phone around so she could

see. She looked down at it, then looked back up at him. It was the only word Ryann had never said to Charlie—a word she never needed to. James must have been speaking to him.

James looked uncomfortable and shrugged again.

2 DAYS

Ryann gazed over at Alexandria, who was typing as usual, curled up next to her on the roof. She picked up Alexandria's notebook and tore out a page.

Alexandria whipped around at the sound and shouted, "Do you *ever* stop destroying my things?"

Ryann scoffed. "It's just paper. Relax, man." She folded it up into a small crane and pulled on the wings so they flapped a bit.

"How do you do that?"

"The master of paper crafts asks a lowly crane-making peasant," Ryann said dryly.

Alexandria frowned. "It's not the same. I use wood and glue to make my mobiles. And how do you know how to do anything like that anyway?"

"Well, when I was younger my mother hired a private tutor—" Ryann started sarcastically, and Alexandria gave her a dour look. "I don't know, man! James learned it at school and taught me or something, but that was years ago." She flicked the crane off the roof and into the garden.

Alexandria stared at it lying there like crumpled-up trash on her lawn.

"Will you show me how?" she asked.

"Sure."

10 MINUTES

The first ones Alexandria made were bent and misshapen. Ryann unfolded the paper and she tried again. And again. And again.

They stayed up until ten past two. When Orion was almost just past view. When Ryann was so tired that she bowed and bent in the breeze like a reed and her sharp edges turned to sea glass.

In the dark of her room, once Ryann had left, Alexandria the Great made a crane as sharp and straight as a pin.

3 DAYS

Alexandria tensed a bit when Ryann set her tray down next to her. And she jolted when Tomas sat down on her other side. Ryann tossed her apple across the table to Ahmed, who caught it and sat down too, like nothing out of the ordinary was happening. Even though their regular table was on the other side of the room.

"So anyway," Ahmed continued, "after we got back, one of Shannon's exes said some wild racist shit about us hanging out and I was wondering if you're interested in getting in on roughing him up."

"I do like fights and it has been a month or two," Ryann said contemplatively. "Let's ask Alexandria what she thinks."

Alexandria looked alarmed to be included in this conversation. "I . . . don't care who Ryann fights," she said slowly.

Ryann poked her fork in Alexandria's direction. "This is why I like her. Savage."

Ahmed didn't look impressed.

"My parents are out of town this weekend," Tomas said tentatively.

"What time is the party?" Ahmed asked.

Tomas looked thoughtful. "Well . . . I've been thinking about *not* trashing my house this time, guys?"

Ryann, Blake, and Ahmed laughed so loudly that some-one threw a dinner roll and yelled for them to be quiet.

"Whew, yeah." Ryann wiped her eyes. "So anyway, when is it?"

"Friday." Tomas sulked. "Alex can come too if she wants."

"Alexandria," Ryann corrected, glancing over at Alexan-dria, who still seemed alarmed. "And yeah. I'll keep an eye on her."

AT THE END OF THE DAY

Alexandria drove Ryann home with her again. She hadn't known that Ryann had been taking the bus all the way across town until she pulled up next to her on the side of the road. So she hopped in and resumed last week's experience of clutching the door as Alexandria swerved all the way home.

"I'm sure we don't have enough in common for you to keep coming after my arm heals," Alexandria said suddenly. "And I definitely don't have enough in common with your friends to be hanging out with them."

Ryann snorted. "You think I have things in common with my other friends?"

Alexandria shrugged.

"The reason we're friends is because we don't have anything in common with anybody," Ryann said. "There was nowhere else to go. Tomas is a huge video game nerd; I can barely keep up with that shit. Even though Blake looks really tough he's super into theater. Travels three cities over just to get covered in grease paint. Sometimes we go see his shows, but it's never been my thing in particular."

She paused for a minute to clutch the side of the car as Alexandria went over a speed bump at thirty-five miles per hour.

"Ahmed is interesting. It took ages for his parents to like me. Shannon is a bit of an outlier. She has all the ingredients for success and is pretty popular. The only weird thing she's into . . . is us. She likes your hair by the way. She wanted to tell you herself but you scare the shit out of her."

"I scare her?" Alexandria spluttered incredulously. "That's ridiculous."

"It's not! You're scary! You can glare straight through a wall. If you told me you could blow up heads with your mind, I wouldn't be surprised."

Alexandria scowled.

"You should talk to her," Ryann continued as they pulled into Alexandria's driveway. "She's the nicest of all of us."

Alexandria brought it up again later, when it was almost time for Ryann to leave. "What is James like?"

"Every time you ask a question, it sounds like a demand. You might as well have just said 'Tell me about James,'" Ryann said. She was lying on her back with her leather jacket half over her face. She had tried to sleep her way through most of the night.

Alexandria didn't respond. Stubbornly waiting.

Ryann sighed. "James is . . . he's . . . secretive. He's a good cook. Messy. Easy to like, I think. Why?"

". . . Is he deaf?"

Ryann pulled her jacket back a bit so she could see Alexandria. The other girl didn't turn to meet her eye, though she probably could tell Ryann was looking at her.

"No," Ryann said quietly. "Something really bad happened when we were younger, and he just stopped talking. Stopped wanting to, I guess." She yawned and pulled the jacket back over her head. "If you took everything about me that's remotely bearable and increased it a hundred times, that's James. My Birdie. Best thing I ever got . . ."

Alexandria started to ask her to tell her more, but Ryann was asleep.

The next day was unseasonably cold.

Ryann woke up with frost on her eyelashes. She rolled over and rubbed her face, then curled into a ball and shivered. She liked colder weather in general, but the mornings were always brutal. She could practically see her breath.

Ryann puffed steam out of her mouth for a while, watching it curl up and fade. Then she sat up and ran into the living room.

Charlie's crib was empty.

Ryann sagged in relief and leaned against the tiny wooden bed. The bed she and James had carried for six miles out from the dump. After all the work and money they'd put into keeping Charlie alive, having him freeze because no one knew the frost would set in early would have been too much.

She went and knocked on James's door and waited for him to knock back against the wall.

James had curled up like an egg around his baby to form a pocket of warmth around him. The covers were pulled up to Charlie's fluffy red hair.

Ryann slid down the side of the bed and sat on a pile of James's jeans. "You want to eat something hot?"

James nodded.

Ryann sighed and got up to go get dressed.

32 MINUTES

Ryann walked about a mile along the edge of the trailer park—past the farthest trailers, past the farthest roads—to where the Papirova apple trees grew.

She hopped the wooden fence and picked about ten apples and shoved them in her bookbag. She tried to get the ones that looked bruised and were closer to white than green. Then she took the apples home.

She peeled the skins off the apples with a pocketknife and left them in a pile on the table. Then she melted some butter and sugar in a pan and grated the apples into mush with a cheese grater. She mixed the apple mash with the sweet butter and added a pinch of salt. Then she poured some cinnamon candy into the applesauce and stirred.

Ryann spooned some of it into a bowl to give to James and put the rest into jars. Then she went back outside, hiked through the woods, hopped over the fence, and left a jar by one of the apple trees. Snug and warm in the fallen leaves.

Ryann hopped down from the skylight early that night. She pulled Alexandria down and immediately went to go check herself out in her mirror.

"You're coming to Tomas's party, right?" she asked.

Alexandria shrugged.

"Tomas complains, but he throws legendary parties. I don't think it's your thing, but you should at least go once." Ryann combed her hair back with her fingers and rubbed at some dirt on her T-shirt. "Don't have time to run home and change . . . ," she mumbled.

"Are you sure he won't mind me being there?" Alexandria asked.

"Dude, Tomas likes you. And even if he didn't, there will be so many people there he might not even see you."

Alexandria tossed Ryann a comb. She caught it, surprised.

"Thanks! Anyway, if you stick by me or James, we'll keep an eye out. If I get too plastered, James's your best bet. Even Shannon will do, if you can find her. Just don't go off on your own unless you think you can handle it."

Alexandria got up and snatched the comb away. "I can handle it," she snapped.

Ryann shrugged, grinning. "I didn't say you couldn't."

48 MINUTES

Tomas did black light like he was getting paid for it.

He'd gotten the walls and ceilings of every room in his parents' mini-mansion blacked out with plastic sheeting. There was new trash furniture he'd probably had trucked in from the dump for people to wreck. There was a trampoline in the living room that some girls were jumping on, and there were buckets of neon paint everywhere. There had to be at least one hundred people in various stages of undress, running at maximum speed and yelling at the top of their lungs while aggressive glitch synth pulsed through the rooms.

Alexandria stood very close to Ryann and stared at the chaos. She looked nervous—which, on her face, came out as looking absolutely murderous.

Ryann grabbed the collar of some hyper-looking freshman who was walking by and yanked her backward.

"Shannon Greenly! Where's Shannon?!" she shouted over the music.

The kid shrugged and pointed to the stairs.

Ryann put her arm around Alexandria's shoulders to keep her from getting bumped, and they both went upstairs.

They didn't have to look for long.

Ahmed skidded across the mezzanine. He was shirtless

and covered in pink neon paint. He had a water gun in his hand, and maybe twenty similarly dressed people were running behind him. He was wearing one of his older turbans, fully preparing to get it messed.

"Ryann!" he yelled. He stopped to bump shoulders quickly in hello, then he threw himself over the balcony and onto the trampoline below.

Ryann peeked over the edge to make sure he was okay, then pulled Alexandria farther into the house.

They found Shannon sitting in Tomas's room with some girl draped over her lap. Shannon clapped happily and reached up to hug Ryann hello. She was very drunk.

"Oh, hey everybody. Ryann'sss here!" she slurred. "And she brought our new friend!"

Ryann flung her arms in the air, and everyone cheered.

Shannon struggled to her feet and draped her arms around a stiff and mortified Alexandria.

Ryann tugged at the back of Shannon's shirt, and Shannon fell back, giggling.

Alexandria turned bright red. She rubbed hard at her cheek and looked up at Ryann, speechless.

Ryann shrugged.

"Don't leave me with these people," Alexandria demanded.

"Don't worry, I'm staying," Ryann said.

53 SECONDS

"You got here just in time, we were just about to start three minutes in heaven," a girl nearby said as Shannon pulled Ryann into the circle. "It doesn't rhyme, but seven minutes is entirely too long."

Ryann glanced over at Alexandria, who was stone-faced and tight-lipped.

"You okay?" Ryann asked quietly.

"I've never played this," Alexandria admitted.

"You don't have to play if you don't want," Ryann said, but Alexandria sat down in the circle anyway.

Carolina Finsky, one of the pom-squad girls, cracked open a beer, shotgunned it, then slammed it down in the middle of the circle. "Here's the rules. Three minutes only. No one cares what you do in the closet. No respins, no fighting, no cheating, and rejections have to pay a penalty." She spun the bottle hard and it landed on a guy named Franklin from Ryann's pre-calc class. Carolina grabbed Franklin by the front of his shirt and dragged him away.

There were about fifteen kids playing, so it took a while to get around to everyone. Ryann was near the end, so she had the luxury of not really having to pay attention unless it landed on her. She turned back to Alexandria. "Did you never go to parties like this at your other school?"

Alexandria shrugged one shoulder. "I've been home-schooled off and on. I didn't get to know people well enough to get invited. And . . . even if they did invite me, I never knew anyone well enough to want to go."

"Oh," Ryann said, pulling at carpet threads anxiously. "Well, Tomas is always happy to have everyone at these things. He seems to really like you."

"Why?" Alexandria asked.

"Hmm. He likes to pick his friends based on how interesting they are, more than how nice they are. No offense."

The corner of Alexandria's mouth tipped upward.

"OHHHHHH!"

Ryann looked up, startled. The bottle was pointing at Alexandria. Across the room, Connor McFarland, Shannon's skeezy ex-boyfriend, licked his lips dramatically and started to get up. Shannon slammed her hand on his shoulder and pushed him back down.

"She's new, give her a break. I'll go with her and be a rule breaker. Whatever," Shannon said curtly. "Come on, Alex."

Shannon grabbed Alexandria's hand and pulled her toward the closet.

"Rule breakers have to take penalties!" Connor crowed, laughing. "You girls gonna let me listen in?"

"Shut the fuck up," Ryann snarled.

Connor rolled his eyes and took a sip of his drink.

"Don't be bitter, 'lezzie.' You'll get the girl someday," he said.

Carolina pushed Connor and shot Ryann a sympathetic look. Ryann silently promised to make Connor regret saying that, when he was sober enough to remember the beating.

Shannon and Alexandria came out of the closet exactly three minutes later. Alexandria's cheeks were lightly pink and Shannon was grinning triumphantly. The other kids cheered, while Shannon bowed dramatically. Alexandria went to go sit back next to Ryann.

"Did you get to kiss her?" Ryann blurted, then immediately wished she hadn't.

Alexandria just snorted. "No, she's just . . . really, really nice."

Ryann started to ask another question, but Connor yelled, "PENALTY! You gotta do a truth or dare, Shannon Greenly."

"Fine," Shannon said, sitting down heavily.

"Truth or dare?" Franklin asked.

"Dare."

"I dare you to do three minutes in the closet with Connor," Franklin said, grinning.

"You dicks are so predictable," Shannon griped. "What the fuck ever. Three minutes of silence and no touching with Connor. Come on."

Ryann watched them go into the closet, then she turned back to Alexandria.

"Yeah, she is nice," Ryann continued. "What did you guys talk about?"

Alexandria shrugged self-consciously and picked at the label on her drink. "She said she liked my haircut and asked me some stuff about myself. Told me some things about you guys."

Ryann chuckled and licked at the rim of her bottle. "Like what?"

Alexandria opened her mouth to reply, but a loud bang against the closet door startled the group into silence. It was followed by panicked scratching and a muffled yelp. Some of the group laughed nervously, but Ryann scrambled to her feet. She strode to the door and knocked on it, but there was no answer. She twisted the handle. It was locked. "Shannon, are you okay?"

When there were just more muffled noises in response, Ryann yanked open a nearby desk drawer and pulled out a letter opener.

"What are you doing?" Carolina asked.

Ryann didn't reply. She jammed the letter opener in the door hinge and hit the end of it with the back of her beer bottle. Then she turned the letter opener roughly until the nails fell out, and then pulled the entire door off the door frame. Ryann froze, blinking, trying to process what she was looking at.

Shannon was thrashing under Connor, trying to push him off her. Her blue eyes were wide with panic. Connor turned, startled by the unexpected noise and light.

Ryann yanked Connor off Shannon and backhanded him so hard his lip instantly split.

Alexandria rushed past her to help Shannon up, but Ryann couldn't concentrate on that right now. She could vaguely hear Shannon gasping through the haze of rage as Ryann kicked Connor in the kneecap to bring him down. She landed hard on his chest and began punching him in the face and throat. He started to push her off, so Ryann curled both her legs over his arms and continued bashing in his face.

After a couple moments of shouting, several hands wrapped around her and dragged her off him.

Ryann turned around, ready to fight whoever was holding her, but it was only a white-faced Carolina and a furious Franklin.

"GET OFF ME," Ryann shouted. "I'LL KILL HIM!"

"You can't—you'll get in more trouble than he will!" Carolina begged.

Franklin let go of Ryann's arm. Then he lunged forward and punched Connor in the side of the head, knocking him out cold.

"Someone get Ahmed," he said, chest heaving. He stared down at Connor in shock. "I'm so, so sorry Shannon, I didn't know he was capable of that."

Ryann snatched her arm out of Carolina's grip and turned to look for Shannon, but she and Alexandria were gone.

11 MINUTES AND 14 SECONDS

Someone called the cops.

Two of them manhandled Tomas up the stairs and waited while he announced that the party was over. Franklin came down the stairs with an even bloodier Connor, who was standing on his own two feet and avoiding eye contact with everyone. He walked past the cops, who only gave him a cursory glance. That made Ryann see red again, and she started after him.

She was almost out the door when one of the officers placed a meaty hand on her shoulder and whirled her around.

"You got anywhere to be, Bird?"

Ryann had a history with cops. She didn't know this one's face, but the officer knew her name, which was never a good sign. The other officer turned his eyes in Ryann's direction as well.

"Heard you've been fighting tonight," he said, narrowing his eyes.

Ryann smacked the cop's hand off her shoulder and opened her mouth to make a big mistake. But Alexandria and Shannon appeared next to her and stopped it.

"We're waiting for my dad to pick us all up. She was just showing me around," Alexandria said, coolly gazing into the officer's eyes.

The second officer's belt creaked as he put a threatening hand on the leather. "And who are you, now?"

Tomas jogged over. "Hey—hey heyheyheyhey. Please, no. I'll give you two hundred dollars each to just let everyone go home. Party's over. Everything's fine, right?"

The cops glanced at each other, then pocketed the cash.

"Last time, kid," the first one said as he jabbed a finger into the center of Tomas's chest. "Or your parents will come back to you in a cell."

They took one last look around the place and then walked out.

"Yeah, thanks, okay. Alwaysnicetoseeyoubye." Tomas closed his eyes and leaned heavily against the door.

7 MINUTES

"Are you okay?"

Ryann reached up to touch Shannon's face, but she flinched away.

"Don't . . . just don't touch her right now," Ahmed said gently. "I heard you savaged Connor and ripped a door off the hinges, Ryann?"

"Yes. And I'll do it again when we get back to school," Ryann promised.

"You can't," Tomas said flatly. "His dad's a cop. Why do you think he just walked out of here like it was nothing? Those ten minutes of justice are the only justice he's going to get, probably."

"I heard Franklin choked him out, too," Shannon said quietly.

"That's not enough—" Ryann started.

"It's not Franklin's fault," Shannon said firmly.

Ryann scowled at that, privately disagreeing, then turned to Alexandria. "Is your dad really coming to pick you up?"

"He'll be here in a bit. He can give you guys a ride home if you want."

"Thanks for the offer," Ahmed said, tucking the ends of his turban in. "But I don't live that far from here."

"Mr. Rossi gonna be mad you're getting in so late?" Tomas asked. "He's a stickler for rules. You should probably stay here overnight and let Ryann and Alexandria head back together. He'd get less mad if you just came home in the morning."

"Why . . . would I do that?" Ahmed deadpanned. "I hate sleeping over in your house."

Tomas leaned against the doorframe. "Well . . . I'm eighty percent sure Shannon is sleeping here? We planned for that because her parents are out of town . . ."

"I don't want to be alone tonight," Shannon murmured. "But, I . . . don't want to sleep here, either."

Ryann started to speak, but Alexandria interrupted her. "You can come home with me."

25 MINUTES

Mr. Macallough glared at Alexandria. Shannon looked embarrassed and shrank behind Ryann until Mr. Macallough could barely see her.

"Are your parents home?" he asked Shannon sternly.

"No. They went to New York for business. They don't let me go to many parties," Shannon admitted quietly.

Ryann could see Mr. Macallough's jaw clench as he tried to hold in a lecture. He unlocked the car doors and didn't say a word as Ryann, Alexandria, and Shannon scrambled inside.

14 MINUTES

Mr. Macallough stalked into his home wordlessly. He grabbed some bedding from the hall closet and put it on the couch, then went into his bedroom and slammed the door.

Alexandria sighed. She picked up the blankets and brought Ryann and Shannon up into her room.

Shannon gazed at the paper mobiles in wonder as she sat down on the edge of Alexandria's bed. "Thank you for having me over," she said politely. "Your house is really pretty."

Alexandria raised a shoulder self-consciously and mumbled a thanks.

"Are you going to get in trouble because of me, after we leave?" Shannon asked.

"That doesn't matter," Alexandria said forcefully. "Did Connor do anything to you that would require us to go to the hospital or get PlanB?"

Shannon laughed—a bit hysterically. "No, he didn't get far enough." She turned her glassy-eyed gaze over to Ryann. "That was clever. The thing you did with the door," she said.

"I should have done it faster," Ryann said.

Shannon tilted her head curiously. "It doesn't matter how fast or slow. It wouldn't make Connor any less likely to assault someone or force boundaries. Don't make things that aren't your fault your fault. Connor is responsible for Connor's actions. It isn't your fault and it isn't Franklin's fault. He didn't take Connor's hands and make them push me against a wall. He just . . . failed to recognize a predator among his friends. He'll know now. He'll do better now."

Ryann and Alexandria sat in the silence of those words.

Shannon got up and lightly touched the mobiles, gently spinning them on their threads. "Ryann told me you guys look at the stars up here . . . can we do that?"

"Yeah," Alexandria said quickly, jumping up to open the skylight.

1 HOUR AND 7 MINUTES

Shannon sat on the roof between them, silently looking up at the sky. She fell asleep quickly.

"For some reason, thinking about what's far away helps prioritize your feelings about what's all the way down here," Ryann said.

Alexandria made a small noise of agreement and looked down at Shannon, whose blond hair was blowing in the wind. "How's Ahmed doing?" she asked.

Ryann shrugged. "He takes things in stride. I know what he looks like when he's angry, and that wasn't it. He seemed a bit sad and guarded. You were with her right afterward. What happened?"

"Someone yelled to find Ahmed, so that's what we did. He was hanging out with some people in the living room but came over very quickly when he saw the look on Shannon's face. He didn't touch her, but he sort of"—Alexandria held her hands up to demonstrate—"he sort of cupped his hands around her face without touching her at all, and she loosely grasped his wrists as he asked her if she was okay over and over and over. She nodded a lot, and then they looked into each other's eyes for a long time, and then they both turned at once and went downstairs."

Ryann chewed on that for a bit. "He doesn't know what happened, then. It's very like him to work on damage control before demanding details. We should go to his house tomorrow."

"Shouldn't we take Shannon home first?" Alexandria asked.

Ryann looked down at Shannon as she slept, curled in a ball. "No. Generally after parties Ahmed's parents make us breakfast. They'll probably be expecting us."

8 HOURS

Ryann squinted against the sunlight and turned over. She pulled the sheets over her head, then she sat up abruptly. This was Alexandria's house and this was Alexandria's bed. She glanced over and was both relieved and disappointed to see Shannon sleeping next to her.

Ryann moved to swing her legs over the side and nearly stepped on Alexandria, who was curled up on the floor.

Alexandria's forehead was pressed hard against the edge of her bookshelf. She'd flopped over, then curled up close, tucking her knees up by her chin. Ryann gazed down at her in a daze.

Alexandria's face looked completely different when she was asleep. Ryann was so used to looking at Alexandria when she was angry that she didn't exactly know how to feel about Alexandria's face when it was soft and tired. She had blue-black bruises deep underneath her eyes, and her short hair was thoroughly mussed. She made a small noise and then chewed on her lip in her sleep.

Ryann snorted quietly. Charlie did that, too. She'd thought that was something only babies did, but apparently not.

Suddenly, Ryann heard a noise behind her. She turned over, startled.

Shannon was sitting up, awake and watching the both of them. She was making an expression that Ryann had never seen her make before. "I'm not—I mean—I didn't want to wake her," Ryann whispered.

"It's too late for that," Alexandria said, waking up. "Are we going to get breakfast or not? I'm starving."

2 HOURS AND 25 MINUTES

Ahmed stared at the three of them for a full minute when he opened the door.

"Okay . . . okay. We're doing this . . . okay," he mumbled, rubbing his hand over his face. Ryann grimaced. Things had been so chaotic and distracting she'd forgotten about explaining Ahmed's circumstances to Alexandria.

Shannon rushed forward and fell into Ahmed's arms. Ahmed cupped her head gently and swayed with her as he gently stroked her hair.

"Sorry I didn't text before we came," Ryann said.

Ahmed opened his eyes and shot Ryann an irritated glare over Shannon's shoulder. Then he glanced back at his house anxiously before stepping onto the porch. "Did Ryann talk to you about my family?" he asked Alexandria, closing the door quietly behind him.

Alexandria shrugged. "Did she need to?"

"Kind of. Especially if she was going to bring you here unannounced." Ahmed scowled in Ryann's general direction.

"I am so sorry," Ryann whispered sheepishly.

"What could be so complicated that we have to whisper on the porch?" Alexandria asked. "I mean, it couldn't be that ba—"

"I have two dads," Ahmed blurted.

"That's not that—"

"—and a mom," Ahmed interrupted. "They're all my parents, and I don't need you saying anything weird or making any weird faces at them or asking questions."

"Like, a stepmom?" Alexandria asked, narrowing her eyes.

"No," Ahmed and Ryann said in unison.

"They're all his parents," Shannon said softly. "They're all together. It's been that way forever, I think."

"So like . . ." Alexandria narrowed her eyes even further. "Is it a secret?"

"No," Ahmed said quickly. "It's just. People talk . . . and they say things about my family . . . and I don't want you in my house if you're not going to watch your fucking mouth."

"I wouldn't bring her if I thought she wouldn't, Ahmed," Ryann said seriously.

"I know, it's just . . . my dad got really upset when he learned people were making fun of me for it. It was a long time ago, like literally in middle school, but still."

"Ahmed," Alexandria said. "I'm not here to make fun of your family. I wouldn't."

Ahmed looked embarrassed. He rubbed his arm and glanced back at the house. "I know I haven't been the nicest to you," he said haltingly. "And . . . you have every right to get back at me. But please, please don't hurt my— They're happy like this and it's hard to explain that . . . It's just . . . I like them this way and they're good parents."

"It's okay," Alexandria said. "You already apologized. Stop griping about it already. If you feed me, we can be friends. I won't say anything weird or make your dads and mom sad."

"Okay . . ." Ahmed nodded. "Okay. Thanks."

"No problem."

CRACKED

Mr. Bateman looked up from his notebook as they walked into the kitchen. Mr. Rossi was behind him at the stove, frying something in a large pan. He was wearing a frilly yellow apron that was clearly Ahmed's mom's and was also way too short for him. Ryann glanced over at Ahmed, who looked even more embarrassed than before.

"Have all of you been thoroughly scolded by my anxious son?" Mr. Rossi said over his shoulder.

Mr. Bateman scowled. "Don't be a dick." He took his reading glasses off and rubbed his eyes. "I know I usually do Saturday Post-Party Recovery breakfast, but my wrists are acting up, so Jack's taking care of it today. Hope you guys like . . . whatever he's capable of making."

Mr. Rossi flipped him off wordlessly and continued scraping at the pan in front of him.

"Um," Alexandria started.

"Oh sorry!" Ahmed interrupted. "This is my . . . friend . . . Alexandria from school. She's cool, Ryann hangs out with her a lot. Alexandria, these are my dads."

Mr. Bateman nodded. "Nice to meet you, Alexandria, you can call me Mr. Bateman, and behind me is Mr. Rossi. The missus is at work right now, but she's Mrs. Rossi, too."

"Why are you all just standing in the doorway?" Mr. Rossi griped. "Sit down. Come on now, Ahmed, you could at least grab some plates; we've raised you better than this."

Ryann, Shannon, and Alexandria sat down at the table with Mr. Bateman while Ahmed started pulling out silverware.

Mr. Bateman tilted his head and looked at Alexandria the way he had when he first met Ryann. Eerily personal, like he was doing some kind of data retrieval.

Then he said, "You're that kid who just moved here with Eferhilde Watts's partner—The Uninaut's widower."

"The what?" Ryann blurted.

"How do you know that?" Alexandria asked, gripping the wood of the table hard. "That's not public information."

Mr. Bateman looked pensive for a moment. "Things happen in this town that are difficult to describe and difficult to live through. It's almost like it's a magnet that pulls things from the periphery that could never exist anywhere else. You are incredibly rare, and now you're here. In this unremarkably remarkable town. In the right place and the right time for whatever will happen. And when it does, whatever it is, I hope it doesn't hurt people, and I hope you win ... if it's a thing you can win, I guess. Also, you look like her. Eferhilde. Not too much, mind you, but there are very few things I don't notice."

Alexandria frowned. "Oh."

Ahmed tossed plates on the table and handed Ryann and Alexandria their silverware. "He's a writer. All writers are weird, just go with it," he muttered. He sat down next to them and eyed his dad warily.

"All people are weird," Mr. Bateman countered. "So. Why are you here, Alexandria? What is here that isn't anywhere else?"

Alexandria looked over at Ryann, who shrugged. This entire encounter felt very . . . above her pay grade.

"I . . . There . . . For some reason, this area amplifies radio waves more than most other places. If you know who I am, you know why that would be important to me."

Mr. Bateman scratched his chin and thought for a moment. "Are you talking to her?" he asked.

Alexandria glanced down at the tablecloth. "No. We can't send any outgoing messages, just receive new inbound ones. She's too far, and our equipment is too weak to send anything that she'd be able to intercept. It's good enough, though. Just to hear from her. Know she's alive."

"I know how that feels," Mr. Bateman said seriously. "I'm sorry."

Mr. Rossi scraped some scrambled eggs and corned beef hash onto their plates and then handed them each an orange.

"Thank you," Mr. Bateman said softly, gazing up at him.

"Always," Mr. Rossi replied. He said it with weight, like he'd given his husband much more than some singed breakfast food.

Ryann smirked and glanced over at Ahmed.

Ahmed put his head in his hands and stared out into the void.

"Anyway, isn't there an observatory a couple miles out?" Mr. Rossi asked, ignoring his son. "Maybe you could see if you could get some help from them."

"It's a NASA headquarters," Shannon said as she poked at her eggs.

"It's a NASA military base," Ryann quickly amended. "I don't think they care what any of us want."

"Well." Mr. Bateman folded up his notebook and picked up his fork. "It's an honor to meet you, Alexandria, best of luck. You're always welcome under our roof. And Ryann?"

Ryann looked up, startled.

"Don't fuck this up."

38 MINUTES

After breakfast, they took a walk and Shannon explained what happened at Tomas's party. Ahmed stared at the sidewalk, tight-lipped and angry as he listened.

"Do you want me to do anything?" he asked when she'd finished.

Shannon shrugged. "There isn't much more you can do. Ryann punched him in the throat. I think she broke his nose and maybe dislocated his kneecap."

"Okay," Ahmed said firmly. "Do you never want to talk about any of this ever again, or do you want to talk about this until you feel better?"

Shannon thought about that for a moment. "I think I'm done talking about it for now. Thank you for asking." She turned to Alexandria. "I took something from your house. I thought you should know."

She pulled the radio out of her pocket.

Alexandria looked irritated, but also just extremely tired. "Why?"

"I figured we could maybe find a better place to listen for recordings. Ryann told me your dad doesn't like when you do that, so I wanted to help. As a thank-you for last night."

Alexandria seemed surprised.

"My brother used to do radio stuff in college," Shannon continued. "He has a better radio, and it has a recorder. He moved out a year ago and left it behind. I don't think he'd mind if we just took it. It's super old, but it's bigger, and probably has a stronger receiver. Plus, it's battery-operated; most receivers of this size need to be plugged in. We'd have to change the batteries every so often, but if we find a good enough place, we could let it record twenty-four hours a day. That way you'll have more time after school to potentially catch messages."

"How would we find any place like that?" Alexandria asked.

Ryann shrugged. "This town isn't that big. We could walk around the whole thing in a couple of hours until we catch a strong signal, then follow it until it's super crisp."

"Would . . . you really spend your Saturday doing that?" Alexandria asked warily.

"Yeah," Ahmed said. "It's important. Or at least more important than anything else we'd be doing today."

1 HOUR

They started in the residential part of town and worked their way toward the woods at the edge. They switched holding the handheld radio between them, depending on whose arm began to hurt the fastest, waiting for that distinctive static. After an hour Ahmed broke down from boredom and started asking Alexandria hundreds of questions.

"How long have you been doing this?"

"Six years."

"Did your dad ever help you?"

"No. He has a bunch of complicated feelings about SCOUT. He doesn't like talking about it."

"Can't you just contact SCOUT and ask them to send you their recordings?"

Alexandria thought for a minute. "No. It's like . . . I guess if SCOUT was NASA it would be easier to get stuff from them because NASA is a government organization. But SCOUT is a privately owned company and all the data they receive they distribute at their discretion. My dad asked once when I was a lot younger, and he told me they said no."

"Did he just tell you that, or did you try again later when you got old enough to check?" Ahmed asked seriously.

Alexandria frowned. "I don't think my dad would lie to me about that."

Ahmed bit his lip as he thought about it. "Parents keep secrets sometimes. Often to protect us. I'm not insinuating that your dad lied to you. It's more of a 'maybe we should just look into it more again' sort of thing."

Alexandria scowled deeper and handed the radio to Shannon, who held it high up in the air.

6 HOURS AND 13 MINUTES

They trudged on until it was nearly sundown and the build-ings gave way to fields and trees. Suddenly the radio—which had been broadcasting light static off and on—crackled loudly. Ahmed shook it to make sure, then they turned to follow the sound. The radio crackled in and out of silence until they entered a vast clearing.

Rising up out of the grove like a monolith were the twisted, charred remains of an industrial warehouse.

"Gross," Shannon said.

"What is this place?" Alexandria asked quietly.

Ahmed grimaced. "A structurally unstable remnant of my dads' criminal past," he said bluntly.

"Why do you think the signal is strongest here?" Ryann asked.

"I don't know." Ahmed threw his arms out in exaspera-tion. "It's probably haunted."

"It can't be haunted," Ryann countered. "Your parents are still alive."

"It might just be well-positioned globally or something," Shannon said. "Don't look a gift horse in the mouth." She pulled her hair into a ponytail. "Okay. Let's go."

Ryann stopped her. "No one should go in there without

hard hats or masks. Plus, we have to get the stronger radio anyway. Let's go back, get some food, get Tomas and Blake, and actually do this safely."

Shannon threw her hands up and sighed. "Fine. Do I have to wear kneepads, too?"

"Yes," Alexandria replied.

Ahmed tossed an arm around Shannon's shoulders and steered her toward the edge of the clearing. "Come on. Let's go back." As he passed Alexandria he nudged her shoulder and smirked. "Glad to have you here as another voice of reason."

Alexandria didn't smile at that, but Ryann could tell she was happy.

2 WEEKS AND 3 DAYS

It took a while to coordinate everyone's schedule, but eventually they all met up after school and trudged out to the woods. Alexandria and Ryann held Shannon's brother's bulky radio between them while Ahmed and Shannon lugged the batteries. Tomas fiddled with Alexandria's old handheld radio as they walked.

"Blake has play practice, but he'll be there to meet us," Tomas explained. "It takes an hour to walk from school to the woods, but his class is only a half-hour drive away so he'll probably beat us there."

"What's he bringing?" Ryann asked.

"Safety supplies," Ahmed said. "Masks and hard hats."

"What did *you* bring?" Alexandria asked Tomas.

"Battery-powered lanterns, a broom, and some gloves." Tomas fingered the broom handle poking crazily out of his bookbag. "I didn't bring any of my school stuff to make sure all this shit would fit."

Alexandria was quiet for a bit.

"Why are you all helping me?" she asked suddenly. "You guys don't have to care about any of this."

Tomas snorted. "What do you think I'd be doing if I wasn't here? I'll give you a clue. It rhymes with 'hitting on my sass and cheeting purritos.' You're the most interesting thing that's happened in this town in months."

"Plus," Ahmed added, "I owe you for the whole Shannon thing. Ryann told me your dad was pissed."

"I *was* the Shannon thing, and yes, he was," Shannon said.

They all glanced back at Ryann.

"I . . . like space," Ryann said quietly. "I didn't think I'd meet anyone else who cared about it the way I used to. I have priorities with James and things got really busy and I just . . . shelved that dream. But when you got here I was like . . . I don't know. It's a good opportunity to do anything I can to help, I guess. It's the closest I'll get to being in that world, I think."

"That's really sad," Tomas said, adjusting the straps of his bookbag.

"You can try," Ahmed said, nudging Ryann with his shoulder. "I know you're shit at math, but you're great at science."

"NASA and SCOUT look for a lot of things in people," Alexandria said. "You could apply."

Ryann laughed bitterly. "Thanks, but it's okay, guys. This isn't about me and I doubt I'll have anything they're 'looking for.' I'm fine."

Ryann could feel Alexandria's eyes on the back of her neck, but she refused to turn and meet them.

1 HOUR AND 11 MINUTES

Blake was leaning against his car, waiting for them, when they finally trudged into the clearing.

"This shit is from my dads' last renovation site, so don't fuck it up," he said, tossing everyone a hard hat and mask while Tomas passed out gloves.

Ryann put hers on and then checked to make sure Shannon's and Ahmed's were on tight. She paused for a minute, then gazed over at Alexandria.

Alexandria gave Ryann a thumbs-up and tilted her head to show that the neck strap was tight enough. Ryann nodded and turned to look at the burned-out ruins.

Tomas took a loud, deep breath, then marched inside. Ryann picked up one side of Shannon's brother's radio and glanced back at Alexandria. "It will be okay," she said, the mask muffling her voice a bit.

Alexandria looked defensive. "I know," she snapped, and then she marched in after Tomas.

Ryann, Shannon, Blake, and Ahmed followed close behind.

The warehouse was charred completely through. The ceiling had collapsed halfway down into the room, and the sky was visible through it, creating an unintentional skylight. The floor was littered with shattered glass, and it was clear animals had taken refuge within the walls.

At the center of the room, it looked like demolition had begun but hadn't been finished. All the large machines had been moved out and walls knocked down, leaving the room open and empty.

"Gross," Blake said. "Are you sure this is where the best sound is?"

"Yes," Alexandria, Ahmed, and Shannon all said in unison.

Blake thought about it for a minute as he stared at the open ceiling. "I guess that does make sense. This is the flattest, emptiest land nearby, and it's not residential. Plus, since the ceiling is off, nothing will block the signal. I guess it's similar to a big empty field."

Tomas had already begun sweeping the glass up and pushing it outside the room.

"Come on," he said. "It's getting late and I'm not going to leave until we have a place to sit down."

WEST

Ryann helped Ahmed and Blake push all the remaining equipment and charred furniture to the edges of the room. Tomas swept all the debris through the opening in the wall.

"Do you think if we boarded that hole up with cardboard, it would stop animals and rain from getting in?" Shannon asked.

"I don't know," Tomas replied. "I might get a leaf blower and see if we could blow some of the dust out. I don't think we'll be hanging out in here much, but—"

"I might," Alexandria said. "It's probably safer than being on a roof all the time. And the reception is really good. Maybe not *every* night, but . . . you know."

Tomas shrugged. "Sounds fair. I'll buy more lanterns and batteries. Maybe a couch or something from Goodwill?"

"Thanks," Ryann blurted.

"Oh . . . uh, no problem." Tomas eyed the jagged edge of the opening in the brick contemplatively.

After they got most of the trash cleared out, Alexandria and Shannon focused on untangling all the wires. Ryann leaned against the wall and gazed up through the skylight at the moon.

"Hey." Ahmed squatted on his heels next to her. "It's a bit late. Is James picking up Charlie?"

"Yeah, he had some test tomorrow and he wanted to get home early so he could study or something."

Ahmed hummed quietly.

"It's weird to be in here," he said.

"Yeah. I guess it is. Would your dads get mad if they knew we were in here?"

Ahmed laughed dryly. *"Oh yeah."*

"Am I allowed to tell the others?"

"Tell us what?" Shannon asked, yelling from across the room.

Ryann looked back at Ahmed, who gestured for her to go ahead.

"Ahmed's dads think this place is haunted," Ryann yelled back.

Ahmed rolled his eyes. "Ahmed's dads burned this place down and therefore have the pretty reasonable assumption that it's dangerous in here," he corrected. *"Ahmed* thinks it's haunted."

"Why did they burn down a building? Isn't that illegal?" Tomas asked. He turned on the last of the lanterns and placed it next to the radio.

"I don't wanna go into their tragic backstory," Ahmed

said. "Let's just go with teenage angst and lack of supervision. The point of the matter is they can't learn that any of us have been in here, or else they'll get all weird and shouty about it."

"Okay. Whatever." Blake put his coat on. "I'm going home. My hands hurt and it's still dusty in here."

Tomas picked up his bookbag. "I'm coming with," he said quickly. "Anyone else need a ride?"

"Yeah." Ahmed scrambled to his feet. "Come on, Shannon."

"There's one more seat," Blake offered. "Alexandria could sit in someone's lap or something. We'd just have to make sure the cops don't see."

"Thanks, but you guys go," Alexandria said, not looking up from the radio. "I'll walk to my car. I want to keep fiddling with this thing."

Blake looked meaningfully at Ryann, who nodded for him to go. He gave her a mock salute and trudged outside.

Ryann listened to the sound of Blake's engine starting up and Tomas laughing loudly before they peeled off into the night.

8 MINUTES

Alexandria's eyebrows were tight with concentration as she fiddled with the wires that connected the speakers to the receiver.

Ryann brushed some soot off the ground and sat down next to her. "Is all this okay?"

Alexandria hmmed noncommittally and fiddled with the wires a bit more.

"I hope my whole thing about wanting to reconnect with space stuff through all this wasn't . . . I don't know . . . insulting?" Ryann said. "I didn't want to make something that happened to you all about me or anything."

"It's already about you," Alexandria said distractedly. "It's about all of us. That's how science works. It takes a village and all that . . . Oh! There it is."

The room filled with that strange, soft, low static that Ryann recognized from the handheld radio.

Alexandria sighed and stretched out next to Ryann on the filthy floor. They both looked up at the moon.

"It's so weird to be both inside and outside at the same time," Ryann said.

"Hmm. What did you think about what Ahmed said

earlier?" Alexandria asked in that demanding voice she used sometimes.

"What? About his parents being arsonists?" Ryann asked.

"No." Alexandria snorted. "He said . . . about my dad and SCOUT. About him maybe withholding information from me. Does he not trust his own parents? They seemed nice enough."

"Its . . . the opposite I think. He *understands* his parents, and I think that makes him understand why they would lie to protect him from some things. He might even think it's a caring thing. A way you care for people. I don't know."

"Oh," Alexandria said. She closed her eyes. "I'll check."

"Check what?" Ryann asked, turning on her side to look at Alexandria. Alexandria's face was calm, like it had been the last time Ryann saw her sleeping.

"Check to see if my dad's keeping things from me."

Ryann hmmed. "Want to do it together?" she asked. "You could blame it on me if we get caught. I'm pretty sure he already doesn't like me."

Alexandria laughed dryly. "He likes you. He just doesn't trust you. And yeah . . . let's . . . let's check."

Ryann stuck out her pinkie. Alexandria looked at it curiously for a second, surprised. Then she huffed dryly again, shook her head, and linked their pinkies together.

3 DAYS

On Tuesdays, Ryann had band with Tomas before lunch.

For whatever reason, every year everyone got the option to choose gym or band. Ryann didn't like that the girls had to wear shorts in gym, so she picked the easiest instrument that was available—the cymbals—and signed up for band.

Tomas, on the other hand, had been playing the cello for eight years and was very talented. However, in true Tomas fashion, he opted to play the upright bass instead this year. The parts were easier and he could lie around slacking instead of actually practicing when they had free-play time.

Today Ryann lay across several chairs in the back of the room next to him while he read something on his phone.

"What did you and Alexandria do after we left the warehouse?" he asked suddenly.

Ryann shrugged. "She told me she was going to check out more stuff about her dad and see if he knows anything about the messages that he might be keeping from her."

Tomas scrolled in silence for a bit. Then he turned off his phone and looked down at her. "Don't you think this whole thing is a bit . . ."

"A bit what?"

"Depressing?" Tomas finished. "Like . . . it was all exciting and stuff meeting her and that whole thing where she's basically a B-list celebrity—"

"But then it turned out she's just a sad girl from a broken home, missing a mom she never met. With no friends, nomading across America, getting chased by the ghost of her birthright?" Ryann interrupted. "Yeah. It's sad."

Tomas frowned.

"But we're all a bit sad," Ryann continued. She reached up and poked Tomas in the cheek. Tomas smacked Ryann's hand away and blushed.

"I don't wanna talk about my backstory," he mumbled.

"You don't have to!" Ryann laughed. "I know the whole thing."

"True, true. Hmm. I want to ask you something—and feel free to say no. But do you think I can come with you guys to listen? At least on this first night since we set things up?"

Ryann drummed her fingers against the side of her cymbals. She liked the quiet of her nights with Alexandria, and she knew that if Tomas became a regular, the others would follow and it would turn into a nightly party.

"I . . . don't know. I'm not the one you should be asking," Ryann said.

Tomas raised an eyebrow at that but said nothing.

2 CLASS PERIODS

Ryann's phone buzzed in her pocket and she nearly dropped a beaker to pick it up. No one ever called these days, just texted, so it had to be some kind of emergency.

"Hello?"

"Hey." It was Alexandria and she sounded weird. "Ahmed was right, he was keeping something from me."

"RYANN BIRD, PUT YOUR PHONE AWAY."

"One sec," Ryann said to Mr. Gonzalez, then covered the receiver. "It's important."

Mr. Gonzalez frowned. "You have one minute or you'll have to take it into the hall."

"Okay, thanks." Ryann uncovered the receiver. "You have one minute. Go."

"Right," Alexandria said. "So, I just learned that my dad used to work for SCOUT. I wanted to wait and look into it with you, but I didn't want to compromise your ability to visit, so I went through his stuff on my own. We can talk about it later."

Alexandria hung up.

Ryann stared at her phone in shock.

LUNCH

Alexandria was standing at the back of the parking lot.

The setting sun lit her hair up in a halo around her head as she waited for Ryann to reach her. Her chin was tilted up in that way she did whenever she was making herself brave enough to handle something. Ryann glanced over at James, who was climbing onto Ryann's bike and looking at her curiously as she walked past him. She shrugged one shoulder in explanation, then turned back to Alexandria.

Suddenly, Ryann was hit with the memory of when she'd first seen Alexandria on her roof, sitting like an obelisk against the dark sky.

She looked different now—softer, more comfortable. But she was sitting just as still as she had that night. Still like she'd been cut out of a photograph and the world was moving around her.

Alexandria wasn't very tall, but she moved like she was meant to be. She looked like The Uninaut's Daughter.

Ryann met Alexandria at the end of the lot.

"Are you ready for a story?" Alexandria said.

"Yeah."

Alexandria unlocked her car door and Ryann climbed inside.

THE NEXT DAY

Shannon and Tomas were already sitting on the grass when Ryann, Blake, and Ahmed finally made it up the hill.

"I have biology right now. Is this some kind of emergency?" Blake demanded.

"Yes," Ryann said curtly.

"Oh, okay, never mind, sorry about that." Blake tossed his bookbag on the ground and crouched down to sit on it. "So . . . why are we here?"

"I have a favor to ask you guys," Ryann said. "You can totally say no if you want, but I'm sure once you know what it is, you'll understand why I'm asking in the first place."

Blake looked skeptical. "Okay . . ."

Ryann took a deep breath. "You guys already know how I'm helping Alexandria with recording radio transmissions, right?"

"Um . . . yeah, obviously." Ahmed narrowed his eyes. "Why . . . What about it?"

"I . . . need some help with something slightly illegal relating to it."

"What kind of illegal?" Shannon asked.

Ryann paused for a second.

"The company who owns all the stuff relating to her mom's mission isn't that far from here. Maybe a two- to three-hour drive. I need . . . I'm . . . Okay, I'm going to start over."

It was very quiet.

Ryann grimaced, but steeled her resolve. "Way back when Alexandria's mom was first recruited, her dad was a part of one of their internship programs. He still has his work ID from it. From what I researched, they're still using the same security system, so his ID might still work. I'm going to see if I can get into SCOUT and get access to the transcripts for the messages her mom has been sending. So Alexandria can have all of them. It's very, very important to me. We won't be taking anything from there but that. But I need help."

"Oh," Shannon said quietly.

Blake opened his mouth to say something, but Ahmed reached across the circle and covered it so he could talk first.

"Wait. Wait, wait, wait, wait slow down," Ahmed said. "You want us to break into a business so you can rob them of some classified-ass information?"

"Yes," Ryann said firmly.

"Are you high?" Ahmed asked. "Are you literally fucking intoxicated?"

Blake licked Ahmed's hand, and he snatched it away with a small screech.

"How long has she been trying to get this information?" Blake asked, narrowing his eyes even further.

"Six years," Ryann said. "She's been staying up trying to manually catch these since she was old enough to know what was going on. If you don't want to help, that's fine, but this is an opportunity she's waited almost a decade to get, and I'm not going to let it pass her by."

"I'll help," Ahmed said, "but it has to be the least illegal part, and I'm absolutely not coming with. I don't care if that part is the most work ever, I'm not fucking up my chances at getting into a good college."

"That's fine, Ahmed, I really appreciate it," Ryann said gently.

"Does Alexandria know?" Shannon asked. "Have you told her you want to do this yet?"

"Not yet," Ryann said. "I wanted to make sure I could do it before I said anything."

Tomas pulled at the grass next to him and tossed a bit of it in the air. "So you need us to work a heist for you. Like a real heist?"

"Yes."

Ahmed sighed loudly. "Does her dad know?"

Ryann didn't know how to respond to that.

"She has the money and the power to just access this in

some other, more reasonable, way. The only reason you'd come to us like this is if you felt like you had to protect something you thought was more valuable than keeping the sanctity of social graces." Ahmed elaborated. "Which, conclusively, must mean that you're intending for Alexandria to keep this from her dad."

"Spoken like someone who spent his entire life in therapy," Tomas said.

Ahmed pushed him. "Therapy is for everyone. Plus, Blake doesn't seem bothered, and that's basically a first."

Blake shrugged. "I think it's worth helping if we can. It's only a few documents. At worst we'll have to get bailed out or whatever, but that's not that big of an issue. Even you, Ahmed. A misdemeanor would get purged from your record when you turn eighteen. That's in maybe four months? Besides, not everyone has to do the break-in part."

Shannon shook her head. "I can't be one of the people who goes with. I . . . My parents wouldn't understand. They're very conservative and I don't know what would happen if I told them why I needed to come home so late. And that's if everything goes absolutely perfectly and we get away with it."

"You could lie," Tomas suggested.

"I could also get caught in that lie, and it would make the situation ten times worse than if I just was honest with them," Shannon replied. "I'm really sorry."

Ryann nodded. "I get it. And it's okay. You guys are react-ing ten times better to this than I thought you would. I'm actually in shock, to be honest."

Tomas looked a little sheepish, so Blake spoke up. "Last year, James asked us if Tomas and I would help him steal Internet from a business on the other side of your yard, so we ran a cord underground for like an acre in the middle of the night. So. You kind of came to the right group to ask about crime stuff."

Ryann stared at Blake in shock. Ryann managed their life insurance money, but James was better at remembering things so he handled their bills. He hadn't said anything about this to her, but she had been wondering how they came up with more spending money around then. She briefly thought about yelling at him, but she was distracted by Blake getting up to leave.

"Don't worry about it," he said. "We'll work on it over winter break."

1 DAY AND 5 HOURS

The next day there was frost on the ground. By noon snow began to fall.

Ryann hoped she didn't have to sit on the roof in a snowstorm, and she silently began dreading the inevitable argument she was probably going to have with Alexandria over it. They'd been spending nights at the warehouse, but it was too cold and wet to stay in, so Alexandria just shrugged and rescheduled them back to her house.

Ryann had detention, so she took the bus over to Alexandria's house afterward. It felt like she hadn't been there in years even though it had only been a couple of days. Ryann walked up the steps and stared at the door before pushing the bell.

Mr. Macallough opened the door. "Where is your key?" he asked immediately.

"I left it at home . . . sorry."

His frown got deeper.

"I promise it's not lost," Ryann said quickly. "I just switched bookbags with my brother because his had a hole, and I left it in the front pocket and he's at home already because it's late."

Mr. Macallough nodded. "Fine. Alexandria's upstairs. She made some bread and it should be in the oven. Grab it and bring it with you when you go up."

Then he disappeared into the house.

8 MINUTES

Alexandria was already opening the skylight when Ryann walked in. She was wearing her coat, and when she saw Ryann was still wearing hers, she nodded in approval.

"Are we really going to sit on the roof in the snow?" Ryann asked.

"Yes." It was firm and nonnegotiable.

Ryann scowled and pulled herself up through the skylight, then she reached down and pulled Alexandria's slim upper body through so she could shimmy up as well.

"If I were more insecure I'd be jealous of how strong you are," Alexandria admitted. "What do you bench? You can almost deadlift me."

Ryann looked over at Alexandria and thought about how light and lithe Alexandria always felt when she hauled her up here.

"I've always been tall and muscular." Ryann shrugged, embarrassed. "It hasn't always been great, but I'm growing into it I think."

"It looks good on you . . . and it's useful, too, I bet," Alexandria said quickly. "Anyway, my dad made a retractable awning out of a couple of my umbrellas for if the weather gets bad. It's pretty cool. It's portable, too, so I don't have to leave it up here."

She tugged at it until it made a small cave, then kicked away the snow on the roof underneath it. "Hey, could you go grab some things from my bed?" she asked Ryann. "There should be two folded-up blankets, a sleeping bag, and a couple Thermoses."

Ryann hopped down and stacked the sleeping bag, blankets, and Thermoses on top of one another and climbed back up. Alexandria arranged the blankets around the sleeping bag and then climbed inside, pulling the food close enough to reach. Ryann sat down on the roof under the awning and pulled out her phone.

"What are you doing?"

Ryann looked up. Alexandria held the sleeping bag flopped wide open.

"Get in," Alexandria demanded. "Do you think I did all this work for my health?"

"You did this for *my* health?" Ryann blurted.

Alexandria went bright red. "Just get in."

Ryann scrunched inside. It was pretty big; there were at least ten inches between them and she could still zip the bag up on the other side.

Alexandria tossed the rest of the blanket over the outside

of the sleeping bag irritably, then fiddled with some buttons on the side until the blanket started warming up.

They sat in the cocoon in silence. Alexandria held her radio in a mittened hand and leaned back against the roof with her eyes closed while Ryann read.

It was warm enough that the snow closest to the canopy began to melt away from it in a circle.

"This isn't as cold as I thought it would be," Ryann admitted.

Alexandria opened one eye and looked over at her. "I've been doing this for years. Did you think I didn't find out all the ways to be up here three hundred and sixty-five days of the year?" She snorted. "What are you reading?"

"I'm trying to figure out how to strengthen our reception of the radio signal."

Alexandria opened both eyes and turned to give Ryann her complete attention. "You can do that?"

Ryann shrugged self-consciously. "Blake's weirdly good at engineering. I'm pretty good at problem-solving. If we work together, we could build something that makes Shannon's radio even stronger."

Alexandria hummed interestedly and closed her eyes again. "You could turn those skills into a lot of things . . ."

Ryann looked down at the dog-eared pages of the library book she was holding. "Maybe."

3 HOURS, 21 MINUTES, AND 17 SECONDS

At midnight, Ryann's phone alarm went off. She looked up from her book and over at Alexandria.

Alexandria was asleep, curled up with the radio clutched in her hand.

Ryann reached over and shook her a bit. Alexandria woke up, gazed over at Ryann in sleepy confusion for a second, then started pulling away the sleeping bag and blankets until she was completely free.

Ryann gathered all the things they'd brought up with them and took them down into Alexandria's room, leaving them in a pile by the side of her desk. Then she stood on the ledge waiting for Alexandria to be ready to be helped down.

She watched as Alexandria lifted her radio up high for a couple seconds more before pocketing it. Then Alexandria came over to the skylight and wordlessly reached out. Ryann lifted her up and then down through the opening. Alexandria braced her elbow on Ryann's shoulder as Ryann moved her.

Her hand snaked through Ryann's hair and down the back of her neck until her fingertips left the sharp angle of Ryann's jaw and drifted back down to her side.

When Alexandria was on solid ground, she stopped and

looked up at Ryann. Her eyes were heavy, her cheeks still flush from sleep. Ryann gazed back down at her.

Neither of them said anything.

Ryann was warm on the side Alexandria had been sleeping near, and cold on the other. She wanted to be even: warm on both, or cold on both. She knew if she stood there any longer she would get there.

Alexandria broke the silence. "Good night, Ryann Bird."

"Yeah," Ryann said, dazed. "Yeah. I'll . . . see you."

And like a coward, she left.

3 DAYS

Ahmed pulled Ryann out of classes in the middle of the day to ditch with him. He drove them out to the edge of town and parked where he usually did, near the edge of the woods.

He was smoking and looking out the window while Ryann read some work for class in the front seat next to him.

"You wanna talk about it now?" Ryann asked after a bit.

Ahmed sighed, filling the car with even more smoke. "My dad's sick again."

"Which one?"

Ahmed gave her a dry look. "August. Stop acting brand new. He's doing that thing where he lies in bed for days, just staring. It never lasts for long—generally about a week." He sighed again and rubbed his eyes like they were itching. "Sorry for snapping at you. It's just . . . Love is such an awful, powerful thing."

Ryann studied Ahmed for a moment, then she took the joint out of Ahmed's hand and put it out.

Ahmed kept staring out the window, blinking sleepily. "My . . . It's almost like they can't breathe without each other. I don't even know what would happen if one of them died," he admitted. "The magnitude of it is terrifying. My dad is fine in a way. He knows what's going on and he weathers it and doesn't feel any less for it. He's not even really sad, just a bit empty for a while I guess, and then he comes back right as rain. But when he's gone, my other dad is in pieces. Sometimes he lies there with him for the whole time. Or they'll take turns and Mom will stay with him for a while and then they switch. Afterward they need a whole day together to heal from it, and my other dad apologizes to me over and over, like I'd ever be mad about it or blame him or whatever."

Ahmed sniffed and rubbed his hand roughly over his face. "I don't ever want to know what it's like to love someone that much," he finished.

"I know," Ryann said. "Me neither."

"You do. You look at people like that sometimes, you know?" Ahmed said, finally turning around. "The way my dads look at my mom when she wears red lipstick, or when she's made their favorite food. Or how my dads look at each other after they've had a really fun argument or something."

"I don't look at anyone like anything—" Ryann started.

"But you *do*," Ahmed interrupted. "Your face is . . . expressive. It's not a bad thing. But you should know that when you like someone, other people can tell . . ."

"Let's agree to disagree."

Ahmed closed his eyes and leaned back against the head-rest. "Whatever. I was trying to help but, whatever. Wanna come over tonight? I'll get my mom to drive you home."

"Yeah, okay."

42 MINUTES

All the lights were off when they came inside.

"They're home, don't worry. Car's in the driveway," Ahmed said, shrugging his bookbag off and onto the kitchen table. "What do you wanna eat?" He wrenched open the fridge. "We've got . . . some leftover Indian food, some other leftover Indian food, some uncooked chicken, a ball of mozzarella, cereal . . ."

"Hmm. Let's put the mozzarella on the chicken and bake it and then have cheese-chicken," Ryann suggested.

"That's . . . not the worst idea." Ahmed took the ball of mozzarella out of the fridge and put it on the counter.

"I hear someone illegally touching my organic, farm fresh, seventeen dollar mozzarella that I drove two towns over to buy from cheese artisans . . ." Mr. Rossi strode into the kitchen. ". . . and using it to make subpar latchkey kid meals. Hi, Ryann."

"Hey."

Mr. Rossi's eyes were red-rimmed, but he smiled back at her like he was fine. "Okay, so I'm not going to leave two kids hungry while I'm around to make them something, so buckle up for . . . whatever I come up with. I'm mostly just good at baking, so let's focus on that."

Ahmed and Ryann sat down at the table and watched Mr. Rossi make fresh pitas from scratch. Then he sliced up the chicken, poured some sauce from the leftovers into the pan, layered a couple thin slices of mozzarella over it, and popped it in the oven.

When it was done, Mr. Rossi slid the bubbling chicken into the still-steaming bread. He garnished it with a couple of sprigs of cilantro and poured them all some grape juice.

"Butter chicken, mozzarella pita pockets," he announced proudly.

"If you can do this, why are you so bad at breakfast foods?" Ryann blurted.

"August makes me breakfast." Mr. Rossi gazed distractedly at the staircase, then grabbed an apple off the counter. "Anyway, just knock when you want to go home and I'll take you. You kids have no idea how lucky you've got it."

5 HOURS

Ahmed's mom got home around eleven and poked her head into Ahmed's room.

"If you want to stay over, that's fine," she said quietly. "But if you want me to take you home, we can go soon."

Ryann sat up tiredly and rubbed her eyes. Ahmed let out a soft snore next to her. They'd been studying, but he'd fallen asleep on the carpet almost a full half hour ago.

She patted the side of his face good-naturedly, then gathered up her things, put on her jacket, and followed Mrs. Rossi out to the car.

Ahmed's mom drove so smoothly that it nearly lulled her to sleep every time. Ryann rolled down the window so the air would keep her awake. She always felt rude sleeping in other people's cars.

"August told me you all have a new friend?" Mrs. Rossi asked.

Ryann nodded. "Her name's Alexandria."

Mrs. Rossi glanced over at her and smiled. "You're a very good friend; she's lucky to have you."

"Thank you," Ryann said sleepily. She watched the streetlights glide by in a bit of a daze.

They drifted from the residential streets and onto the

highway. Mrs. Rossi turned on the radio to the Top '50s Pop and rolled her window down even though it was getting cold out. "Thanks for coming by tonight. I'm glad Ahmed has you to look after him."

Ryann yawned. "Ahmed looks after himself."

Mrs. Rossi laughed. "So he does. But it's always nice to have someone to lean on. I just thought you should know that we appreciate it. We're happy, but it's hard sometimes."

"I know what that's like."

Mrs. Rossi looked over at Ryann with her deep brown eyes, owlish and wise. "I know you do."

They rode in silence until the trees grew thick beside the roads and the noise from the city faded into the dark. Ryann checked her phone to see if James had texted, but he hadn't.

Ahmed had sent her a quick good-night and a bunch of peace signs.

Mrs. Rossi pulled into the trailer park and drove all the way up to Ryann's house, over the gravel and overgrown weeds, even as the car jolted and heaved.

Ryann liked riding home with Mrs. Rossi because everyone else always let her out at the front gate, and it felt a bit luxurious to walk straight from a car right into her home.

She rubbed her eyes again and unbuckled her seat belt.

"Hey, one more thing," Mrs. Rossi said before Ryann got

out of the car. "Don't . . . take time for granted. You have all this freedom and opportunity and people around who love you. Make sure you use the time you have to love them back. I know you know that, but I just thought that someone should say it to you out loud."

Ryann's sleepiness made her bold. "Is that why you and Mr. Bateman and Mr. Rossi can make it work?" she asked.

Mrs. Rossi smiled softly. "Something like that. Now go home, Ryann Bird. Your family is waiting."

Ryann went straight home after school the next day. Alexandria was out of town—something family-related—so Ryann would have felt weird being at her house while both she and her dad weren't there.

She hadn't been home straight after school in so long that she wasn't quite sure what to do with all the time. She cleaned up her room and vacuumed the rest of the house. Then she packed lunches for herself and James for the following week and started doing laundry by hand in the sink.

James had been glancing at her curiously all night.

"What?!" she snapped when she couldn't take it anymore.

James glanced over at Charlie sleeping and narrowed his eyes at Ryann.

"What?" Ryann asked more quietly, but just as vehemently.

He pulled his phone out. *You should use this extra time to study more. I saw you reading that book about radio waves for Alexandria.*

Ryann gaped at James angrily. "I'm not studying for Alexandria, Jesus Christ. We're graduating in a few months anyway and you know I'm not going to college. I have to start working. We're getting low on savings. You can't eat grades."

James scowled and typed back. *I wasn't talking about that.*

You need to study for yourself. You're so focused on her that you're missing out on the fact that everyone else is focusing on you.

Ryann scowled.

James continued. *You're smart. We can figure the money thing out. You can take out student loans and we can illegally stay in your student housing or something, I don't know. But what I do know is that you cared a lot about following in Mom's footsteps before and I'm sure you still do. Alexandria knows that too, or she wouldn't have let you keep sticking around. I can tell you were wondering that while reading. You should control your face better, loser.*

He typed *You're smart* again for emphasis and encouragement. Then he kissed Ryann's knuckles and gently bopped the side of her face. *Now go do it, star-kid.*

"Yeah, yeah. Love you, too." Ryann rolled her eyes. "Even when you're being a dick."

James grinned.

MONDAY MORNING,
AND THEN, AFTER SCHOOL

When Alexandria got back, Ryann told her about what she had asked Blake, Ahmed, Tomas, and Shannon to do. Alexandria pressed her lips together pensively and was quiet. Then she asked to meet with Ryann to talk about it more after school.

Alexandria came up beside her in the hallway, after eighth period had ended. "Are you sure about all this?"

Ryann looked up at her, then continued stuffing things into her bookbag. "No, but I think it's a good time to try." She swung her bookbag onto her shoulders. "Coming?"

Ryann walked with Alexandria out into the parking lot and got in her car.

"It's a good time for something like this, I guess," Alexandria said. "We have a lot of resources at our disposal and we have all winter break to plan."

"If your dad finds out, he will literally kill you. Kill us," Ryann corrected. "Both of us."

Alexandria snorted. "If we get put in jail he absolutely won't bail us out, that's for sure."

"Tomas would," Ryann said. "He's independently wealthy—which still feels weird to say. His parents are loaded, yeah, but his inheritance is from his grandpa and he got it maybe a year ago. Also, unless we do it before January, he can't come with because his birthday is on New Year's Day and he'll be tried as an adult for whatever it is they'd charge us with."

Alexandria laughed quietly. "You guys are all so weird."

"You're weird, too," Ryann joked.

Alexandria didn't reply, but her brown cheeks flushed prettily.

Ryann snatched her eyes away from Alexandria and looked out the window. Her heart pounded against her ribs. *Okay. Okayokayokayokay.*

Alexandria parked at the edge of the woods and got out of the car. She tapped on the window, startling Ryann out of her panic attack.

"You interested in getting out at some point this century?" Alexandria asked.

Ryann scrambled up and out of the car and followed Alexandria into the burned-out warehouse.

When they got inside, it was clear that Tomas had been in there without them. The concrete had been mopped, and there was a large rug that Ryann recognized from Tomas's basement placed under the radio for them all to sit on. Blake had been there, too, if the wood board he'd tacked up to close off the wall was any indication. He'd also left a giant plastic crate of batteries in the corner and cut a hole in Tomas's rug so he could weld the radio to the ground to avert thieves.

"Wow . . . ," Alexandria gasped.

"Tomas and Blake were here," Ryann said. "I don't think anyone else came with them. I know Ahmed wanted to do something about that rubble in the corner, but it's still here . . ."

Alexandria sat down on the rug next to the radio. She took out the thumb drive and replaced it with a blank one.

"I wish we could have a fire or something," she said.

Ryann thought for one alarming second about what Alexandria's face would look like lit by firelight—all shadows and sharp planes. Red and gold and honey-brown. She swallowed and glanced over, but Alexandria was fiddling with her Galaxy Switch.

"I can do that, actually," Ryann said. "If you want, I can

make it for you. A fire. I can make you a bonfire."

Alexandria raised an eyebrow. "Wow, really? You're very handy, you know that?"

Ryann had no idea what expression she was making, but her face felt super hot, so she opted to escape outside to go collect firewood.

18 MINUTES

Ryann hadn't had a crush on anyone for years and she'd almost completely forgotten what it felt like. She'd had a bit of a thing for Tomas maybe three years ago, but after the humiliating event of asking him out and having him stare back at her in shock, then loudly whisper, "I thought our friendship was a Gays Only friendship," she'd pretty much just blocked out that entire concept.

There had been the agonizing solid half hour of her explaining that she was mostly attracted to girls, but that Tomas somehow managed to override that. Then there was an additional twenty minutes of Tomas promising that if he was going to date any girl, it would "totally be her," but even though she was "delightfully butch" and "super ripped" she just wasn't . . . a guy.

The entire episode had been so scarring that she hadn't thought about anyone else romantically until this whole . . . thing . . . with Alexandria slammed into her from behind.

So now, here she was! Gathering branches in the freezing cold. While lights flashed off and on behind her eyes and the devil himself bashed a pan with a spatula while screaming, "WELCOME TO HELL! WELCOME TO HELL!" in her ear.

Did Alexandria even like girls? There was literally no way

to ask that without Ryann showing her own hand before she was ready. And even if Alexandria did, who said that she'd want to be with Ryann, of all people?

Alexandria was tiny and pretty and Ryann was giant and scarred. And plus, there was that one time with Shannon in the closet and Alexandria had seemed so happy. Shannon looked like she could be an actress or a model, Ryann looked like she hauled lumber or something. They weren't even in the same league. Anyone who liked Shannon couldn't possibly find Ryann attractive.

The hysteria prickled her eyes with tears, so Ryann stopped and took a few deep breaths. She looked down to find her arms filled with branches, so she began trudging back toward the warehouse.

When she got inside, she noticed that Alexandria had made a pile of gravel about a yard away from the rug.

"That was a long time. I almost assumed you weren't coming back," Alexandria said. "I figured we'd need some kind of barrier so we wouldn't just have fire on some branches on concrete."

Ryann nodded, not yet trusting herself to talk and have her voice not come out all strangled.

She piled the sticks on the ground, then framed the entire thing with some beams left over from the abandoned construction. "D-Do you have a lighter? I don't smoke and it just occurred to me that we can't have a fire unless—"

"Yeah." Alexandria pulled one out of her pocket, lit a stick, and tossed it onto the pile.

They sat down next to the radio and settled into an increasingly uncomfortable silence. Ryann kept her eyes forward and scrolled through the Internet on her phone.

Alexandria stared up at the sky. "I used to," she said suddenly.

"What?"

Alexandria sniffled, then wiped her nose. "I used to smoke."

"Oh. Why did you stop?"

"I didn't want to die anymore." Alexandria closed her eyes. "I . . . used to live in a city and a lot of people knew who I was. People used to follow me. Reporters. Sometimes gossip columnists. I was never really a normal kid to them. I mean, obviously I wasn't a huge celebrity, but it happened just often enough to remind me that I didn't own my own history. After a while I couldn't think about anything other than escaping, one way or another."

Ryann pulled her knees up to her chest and rested her head on her arms. "When did you stop?"

"A couple of weeks after I got here," Alexandria admitted. "I realized that there was no one around who thought about me the way everyone in the city did, and it was enough of a relief to . . . you know. Stop using it as an escape."

Ryann didn't know what to say. There was so much about Alexandria that she hadn't understood until right now.

Alexandria sighed. "When Shannon and I were in the closet, she told me that if I stuck by your side, you'd take care of me. But I don't know if that's a good thing. You're taking care of a lot of people already."

Ryann closed her eyes. She could feel the weight of Alexandria's gaze.

"What I'm asking you and your friends to do for me . . . with me. It feels like it's too much," Alexandria finished.

Ryann opened her eyes and turned to face Alexandria—and God she wished she hadn't—because Alexandria had eons in her eyes. But it was too late to look away.

"We all can make our own choices," Ryann said haltingly. "Ahmed, Blake, Tomas, and Shannon all chose this—you . . . helping, I mean. And as for me. If you . . . *If* . . ." She restarted, and said firmly, "If you need someone, I'll be there."

"Promise me," Alexandria whispered. "Pinkie promise me."

Ryann held up her pinkie. Alexandria linked their fingers together and squeezed.

"Okay," Alexandria said, sounding strangely out of breath. Her brown eyes were bright. "I've never trusted anyone like this before, but okay."

Ryann huffed a nervous laugh.

Alexandria grinned back. "This . . . feels so serious," she said.

Ryann's chest tightened with fondness. "Yeah. It does."

MID-DECEMBER

Their school didn't do homecoming anymore. Some incident a couple years back had razed the playing field practically to the ground. So instead they had a winter dance right before letting everyone off for break.

Attendance was mandatory, but tickets were free. The student council generally planned the whole thing themselves and did a bake sale to afford decorations. The art department was responsible for setting everything up, and the shop classes and tech students were responsible for arranging the gym space and handling music and speaker setup.

This year's theme was the eighties, if the posters were anything to go by.

Ryann and Alexandria were helping Shannon tape those posters up in exchange for being let out of class to do it.

The dean had narrowed her eyes at the three of them when they went in to get the forms signed to excuse them from classes. She looked between Shannon, standing there beaming in her pom-squad top and hip-hugger jeans with her blond curls in a bright orange scrunchie, to Alexandria, dour in monochromatic gray, and finally to Ryann hulking next to them in her leather jacket, sweatshirt with thumb holes, and T-shirt that had clearly seen cleaner days.

"I didn't know you were friends," she said, sitting back in her chair. "Are you sure no one else in the pom-squad wanted to help with this?"

Shannon frowned. "I eat lunch with Ryann every day? I'm dating her best friend? Alexandria is new. Is she not allowed to help with dance activities? Aren't we supposed to be welcoming to new students?"

The dean pursed her lips at that, then signed their paperwork and handed it over. "Thought there might be a bullying situation going on. Carry on. Don't vandalize any of the posters."

"I'm not a vandal," Ryann snapped.

The dean hmmed in disbelief, and Ryann almost stepped forward threateningly, but Shannon grabbed Ryann's arm and pulled her out of the office.

16 MINUTES

"What a bitch," Shannon seethed. She slapped the first poster up in the hallway outside the office. "They tell us not to judge a book by its cover, but then, like, they say mean things like that."

"You have to learn to not care, you know?" Alexandria replied, cutting the tape with her teeth.

"Or at least be able to defend yourself well," Ryann mumbled.

Shannon frowned deeper. "You can't always hit people into respecting you, Ryann. It's working for now, but when you turn eighteen it's called battery and assault."

Ryann laughed at that. Not because it was wrong, but more because it was Shannon saying it.

"It's not funny!" she griped. "I don't want to have to visit you in jail."

"You'd visit me in jail?" Ryann teased. She finished taping the poster up and hopped off the chair she was standing on.

Shannon huffed, irritated. "Of course, I'd visit you in jail. Maybe only for the first couple of years, but I'd definitely try."

They continued down the hall, putting up posters every couple feet. Ryann carried the ladder and Alexandria held the posters while Shannon did most of the taping.

"So . . . do you know who you're going with and what you're wearing?" Shannon asked nonchalantly.

Ryann shrugged. "I used to go with Ahmed, but I'm assuming he's taking you this year. I might ask Tomas. At least he's taller than me."

"What are you going to wear?" Shannon asked. "Are you going to wear a costume?"

"Probably not." Ryann laughed. "Maybe Tomas could wear a dress while I wear a suit or something. I still have one of my dad's old ones."

Shannon stopped taping and put her hands on her hips. "You're not wearing an old suit designed for a forty-year-old man to your senior year winter formal. You can come over to my house and borrow something of mine."

"Shannon. You're like . . . half of me. And you wear pastels," Ryann said bluntly.

"I've never been to a school dance," Alexandria admitted quietly.

Shannon gasped. "Let's change that. Just tell James you'll be late for dinner, Ryann. We're all going to my house after school," she said firmly. "Nonnegotiable."

AFTER SCHOOL

Shannon's house was almost as big as Tomas's. Ryann had only been here a few times because Shannon's parents didn't like her. They had come home a couple years back and walked in on her and Shannon studying and thought Shannon had snuck a guy in through her window, and they kicked Ryann out.

When they learned Ryann wasn't her boyfriend and they couldn't bar her from being around for that reason, they settled on calling her a bad influence as many times as possible. Which was hysterical because Shannon drank and smoked way more than Ryann did. Ryann also suspected they didn't know about Ahmed, but she didn't want to poke at that in case it was a sore spot. She didn't know evangelical policy on dating Sikhs, but it probably wasn't great.

Shannon led them upstairs and past her bedroom to a room Ryann had never been in, down the hall.

"My brother, Simon, left all his stuff here when he moved out for college," Shannon explained. "He was super into theater and did a lot of shows with the same place Blake goes to. He kept most of his costumes and he was about your height, Ryann. I figure you might be able to find something that works for you here better than anywhere else."

Simon's room was almost completely wallpapered with

posters cut out from magazines and playbills. It was the only room in Shannon's house that wasn't immaculate.

Shannon pushed into Simon's closet and started tossing things on the bed. "I don't know what you're looking for exactly, but at least his stuff will fit."

Ryann was distracted by the sheer intensity of what she'd just walked into. She pointed at a picture that had been stapled right into the drywall. "Who is that?"

Shannon popped her head out of the closet. "Uh . . . I think . . . oh! Adam Ant. I was going to say Boy George, but I'm pretty sure that's Adam Ant."

"How do you—how is all this stuff here? What is your brother even like?" Alexandria asked, dragging her hands across all the posters. Some of them were even signed.

Shannon was stuffing her hair under a tall, white George Washington wig. She had a bunch of bangles on her arms and a silk vest on over her pom-squad uniform. "Hmm. Kind of like Tomas, but funnier."

Ryann touched the edge of a naval waist jacket. "Your parents were okay with this? I mean . . . I've met them, so that's a valid question."

Shannon sat on the edge of Simon's bed and shrugged a bit. "Simon's a lot older than me, so I don't remember much about how my parents talked to him when I wasn't around.

But he spent a lot of time with me and taught me a lot of cool stuff. I think I started hanging out with you guys because you and Tomas reminded me of him and I missed him. I hope that's not weird."

Alexandria smirked. "I wondered about that, but it seemed rude to ask. You're really different from the rest of the people in this friend group."

Shannon flopped backward onto the bed. "I also thought Ryann looked so cool with her jacket and her motorcycle. Walking around like an absolute dreamboat, yelling at people and breaking things. She's so pretty, right, Alex? It's not fair."

Ryann laughed. "Watch it, you might make Ahmed jealous," she said, frantically trying to divert the subject away from what Alexandria thought about how she looked.

"Ahmed doesn't care," Shannon said. "He's not possessive, you know? Hey, try that jacket on the right—yeah, the red one. If you're going for Adam Ant's look, it would fit better than the navy one." Shannon pointed into the closet, and then hopped up, opened one of the side drawers, and started digging around in it.

"If you're going to do Adam Ant, you've gotta do Adam Ant makeup," Alexandria said, leaning against the door frame.

"I don't know how to do fancy shit. I'm barely accomplishing eyeliner," Ryann replied.

Alexandria shrugged. "I could help. Maybe."

"That sounds like it's going to take a while," Shannon said. "I'm going to see if Simon has anything in Alexandria's size and root through my closet. You know where things are, Ryann. My makeup box is in my room by my desk. Just holler if you need anything."

6 MINUTES AND 21 SECONDS

Ryann sat on Shannon's desk chair and pulled her bangs back into a short ponytail on the top of her head. Alexandria dropped Shannon's large makeup bag onto the desk and then hopped up to sit next to it. She tucked her toes around the legs of Ryann's chair and pulled it closer until she was able to comfortably reach Ryann's face.

Ryann folded her arms, anxious about the closeness.

Alexandria reached out, but Ryann flinched and slid farther down in the chair. She silently willed her heart to stop banging so loudly.

Alexandria rolled her eyes. "Don't move. You'll mess me up."

She daubed a brush around in a container, then reached out and started painting a line down Ryann's forehead.

Ryann had never done this before and she wasn't sure where to point her eyes. She could feel Alexandria's breath on her face and the brushstrokes tickled a bit.

Alexandria being this close made her a little bit dizzy. The heat of Alexandria's thighs was seeping through the sleeves of the jacket Ryann was wearing. She shifted a bit, but Alexandria clicked her tongue in disapproval and steadied Ryann's chin with her other hand.

Ryann thought about how Alexandria looked a few

months ago. With her head tilted back, exhaling into the cold air, her eyes half-lidded, lashes thick and dark. The way she looked at Tomas's party: furious and out of her depth, strobe lights bending around the angles of her face.

How she could smell the familiar scent of Alexandria's house on Alexandria's jean jacket.

Alexandria bit her bottom lip as she worked, her eyebrows creased in concentration. She brushed her thumb against the side of Ryann's cheek, then tilted her face up. "Close your eyes."

In the darkness, Ryann felt dry pencil scraping across her eyelids, followed by more brushing. There was a flurry of soft puffs on the apples of her cheeks and then a spritz of liquid over her whole face that made her flinch.

"There."

Ryann opened her eyes. Alexandria's gaze darted over Ryann's face, searching for something. Ryann instinctively leaned forward. Alexandria didn't pull away. Instead she raised her hand and slipped the band off Ryann's hair, letting it fall softly over her eyes. Ryann let out a breath she didn't even know she was holding.

Shannon opened the door. "I have a Madonna bra and this sequin thing," she said loudly. "Pick which one you want, Alex."

"The sequins," Alexandria and Ryann both said at once.

Alexandria went bright red and hopped down from the desk. "I have to go home."

"Okayyy," Shannon said, suspiciously looking between them. She tossed the dress to Alexandria, who shoved it in her bag. "See you at the dance."

Alexandria rushed out of the room.

"Hope it fits . . . ," Shannon called after her.

Shannon and Ryann got ready at Ahmed's house.

"Why are you two together? Don't you guys want to be surprised when Shannon comes out in her dress and walks down the stairs?" Mr. Rossi asked as he leaned against the wall and watched Shannon do Ryann's makeup. "Like in every teen prom movie ever?"

Ryann shrugged and Shannon made a noise of derision.

"I'm more interested in seeing what Ahmed is wearing," Shannon replied. "He already knows what I'm wearing; I was with him when I got it. Plus, eighties dresses don't make anyone look good."

Mr. Bateman walked past the bathroom door. He did a double take, then walked backward and stuck his head in the doorway. "Who are you supposed to be?" he asked Ryann. "Some kind of . . . Native American, Revolutionary-era, pirate . . . dominatrix?" He narrowed his eyes critically.

"No. She's Adam Ant," Shannon shot back irritably.

Mr. Bateman held up his hands defensively. "Not sure who that is. The eighties must have been a darker time than I remember."

Mr. Rossi snorted. "You were six in the eighties. They're kids. Let them have fun."

"Speaking of which, if you laugh, I swear to God," Ahmed said as he rounded the corner.

His turban was black and he had painstakingly drawn an eyeliner mustache over his mouth. He had on a white tank top tucked into the tightest jeans Ryann had ever seen him wear. He looked very uncomfortable. He wrenched a pair of silver aviators out of his airtight pockets and put them on.

"Oh my God," Ryann and Mr. Bateman blurted simultaneously.

"Freddie Mercury!" Shannon shrieked. She rushed to Ahmed and flicked at one of his tank top straps.

"Ow!" he cried.

"You look great," Shannon said. "This is great. Put on your coat; I want people to see you two looking like this."

DECEMBER 18

They ran into James outside. Apparently, Tomas had showed up as Madonna, but someone made the mistake of saying something to him about it. So he knocked them unconscious and was instantly kicked out, dragging Blake—who came as Sebastian Bach—along with him. James told them that those two were now on the hill. Shannon still wanted the full-fledged Winter Dance Experience, so Ahmed and Ryann went in with her for a while.

They tried to have a good time, they really did. But the music was too garish and the dancing was repulsive. There were balloons everywhere, so you had to kick a path for yourself if you wanted to get anywhere. Some idiot spiked the punch with whiskey, so the teachers dumped out the punch bowl. It was so hot and everyone was so thirsty, people began drinking out of the bathroom sinks.

Ryann kept having to field dance invitations. Apparently, not being in her leather and having her hair away from her face made her far too approachable—something she rapidly began to resent. She wandered around the auditorium looking for Alexandria, but no one seemed to know if she was there or not.

After about an hour, she slipped out the back door and made her way to the hill.

Tomas spotted her and hooted, waving. He lifted a bottle of what looked like rosé in the air.

Ryann grabbed it and took a swig, and then handed it over to Blake—whose costume looked extremely last minute.

"Where are Ahmed and Shannon? They get lost on the way over?" Tomas joked.

Ryann shrugged. "I wanted to give them a proper time at the dance alone together, you know?"

"You just like someone else." Tomas draped his arm over Ryann's shoulder drunkenly and readjusted his wig. "You're so tragic."

"You're lucky I like you," Ryann threatened.

"*You're* lucky I like *you*," Tomas teased, giggling.

"How's your hand?" Ryann asked. "Let me see."

Tomas showed Ryann his bruised knuckles. "Caught his ear. I was aiming for the throat, but he tried to dodge it," he explained.

Ryann clicked her tongue in sympathy and rubbed gently at the red spot. "Where's Alexandria?" she asked.

Blake rolled his eyes.

"I asked her if she wanted to save her first dance for you, but she pushed me and then went home," Tomas said. "She can't take a joke at all. You guys deserve each other. You're both made of layers."

"Layers?" Ryann said dryly.

Tomas hiccupped. "Firssst layer is the asshole layer. You gotta crack that one first. Second layer is the nice one. You think that's the last layer, but it's not 'cause there's another layer under that and its just more asshole. But if you like . . . puushhhhh your hand inside that layer, you know what's in there?"

"What's in there, Tomas?" Ryann tugged the bottle out of Tomas's hand and put the cap on. She had to get this guy some water.

Tomas wasn't done. He swayed dangerously and poked Ryann hard in the chest with one finger. "Fear," he said, entirely too loudly. "You're both chickens with layers. Onion chickens. *I'm* not a chicken."

"No, you're not, Tomas," Ryann said indulgently, patting him gently on the cheek. He slumped over her shoulder and she just barely caught his dead weight as he fell asleep.

She turned to Blake. "Repeat any of that and you'll regret it."

Blake just crossed his arms and looked unimpressed. "She looked good. Sorry you missed it."

Ryann gritted her teeth and wished for the hundredth time that she wasn't so transparent.

2 DAYS

On December twentieth, the last day before winter break, they gathered in the library. They all sat on the floor in the back where there were old textbooks and travel guides. Tomas and Shannon brought their laptops, Ahmed had his tablet, and Blake had shown up empty-handed.

"I'm not sure what I can offer you," he said, tossing his book-bag on the floor. "But I didn't want to be left out of the loop."

Ryann nodded. "Thanks for coming."

Alexandria placed her dad's SCOUT door pass on the floor in the middle of the circle.

"Okay. So. We only have one of those," Ahmed said. "How are we going to make this work?"

"The ID has a PIN associated with it . . . which we guessed—my dad's not creative," Alexandria said. "If we go to the website, we might be able to log in as an employee and get access to their database in some way."

"Have you tried yet?" Ahmed asked.

"Yeah," Ryann said. "The PIN still works, but you have to be using the network from one of their buildings in order for the website itself to allow us in. So when you type in the PIN, it begins to open the webpage, but then a pop-up kicks you out, saying something about security clearance. Username is the first four letters of his first name, first four letters of his last name, no spaces."

She handed the ID to Ahmed, who tried to access the website from his tablet. He passed the ID to Shannon, who tried as well, and then to Tomas, who tossed it back on the floor without even trying.

"Do you know what kind of security clearance this used to have?" Tomas asked.

"I think he used to do some kind of secretarial work, so the clearance probably isn't very high. It might be enough to access his old employee email though, which could give us the opportunity to request permissions updates from IT—" Alexandria started.

"Companies like SCOUT have way too many employees for anyone to be keeping track of who still works there," Shannon interrupted. "I think we have a pretty good shot at being able to get the information sent to us if we ask professionally enough."

"Who would we ask?" Alexandria said. "It's not like we know the internal structure."

"All their staff is available on LinkedIn," Tomas said.

"Okay," Ryann said. "Get all the names of the people in their records department. It will be helpful to be able to rattle off names of staff we know to build trust with other people there if we're caught. The hard part will be getting into the building before we can even use his email address to do any of the rest of this."

"We're really doing this, huh?" Ahmed muttered.

"If you want out, that's okay," Ryann said quietly. "But we need full commitment." She glanced over at Alexandria, whose dark eyes watched her curiously.

"No," Ahmed said, "I mean, like—we can't just stroll in there during the daytime and be all, 'Hey, guys, who am I? That's not important. Mind if I use your network?' We would have to break in, and it would have to be at night. What would we do if we got caught?"

"Uh. They call the cops and we get arrested. Duh," Blake said.

"I'll post bail. If they give us that option," Tomas offered.

"Well the cops have to *get there first*," Ryann pointed out. "It's not like NASA, where breaking in and accessing withheld data is some kind of military crime. It's a private business; they can't detain us. We'd have to wait for the police to get there. But yeah, we'd all leave this scenario with records. Which may or may not disappear when we all turn eighteen— which is something to think about. That said, who wants to come for the actual break-in?"

It was quiet. They all looked at one another anxiously.

"I'll go," Blake said unexpectedly. "Tomas can't bail anyone out if he's in jail himself. Ahmed, you should stay, you can't afford to have priors if you're going to need to get scholarships and stuff. Plus, you won't be alone in bailing. Shannon's parents would send her to boarding school or murder her if she got caught."

"So. Just me, Blake, and Alexandria," Ryann said.

"Less people is less liability," Alexandria pointed out.

"Okay . . . okay. That's true." Ryann sighed. "Tomas, you should drive up with us just in case, so that we have someone we know nearby."

"Sure." Tomas nodded.

"So," Ryann said firmly. "Let's meet up again about this near the end of winter break. We have two and a half weeks. I want to do it at least a week before school starts in case anything goes wrong. Got it?"

"Got it, chief." Tomas closed his laptop as Ahmed and Shannon nodded.

"Yeah, all right." Blake put his bookbag back on. "I'll work on trying to figure out if we need to bring anything."

"Hey," Alexandria said.

Blake looked back over his shoulder at her.

"Thanks."

"Don't mention it," he said.

3 HOURS

Ryann sat down to dinner and pretended there was nothing going on. James bounced Charlie on his knee as he ate spaghetti and watched her warily. He had to keep moving the fork out of Charlie's grasp and was starting to seem irritated.

Ryann finished first and pulled Charlie out of James's lap so he could eat undisturbed. As soon as the baby was gone, James pulled out his cell phone, typed quickly, and pushed it over. *What's about to happen?*

"Nothing."

Don't lie to me. I don't like surprises. James raised an eyebrow, crossed his arms, and waited.

"Blake, Tomas, Alexandria, and I are going to break in to SCOUT to see if we can use Alexandria's father's ID to get access to transmission files SCOUT has been keeping from Alexandria's family."

All the blood drained out of James's face. He snatched up his phone. *WHY?*

"Because this is important to me—to her," Ryann quickly corrected.

James's eyes narrowed at the slip. He tapped his fingers rapidly against the table and bit his lip. *You're going to do this whether I like it or not.*

Ryann stared at the words on James's phone and didn't say anything. She bounced Charlie on her lap. "If . . . ," she started slowly, " . . . you tell me no, I will respect that and stand by my word not to go. But I can't promise that no one else will go, and I can't promise that I won't stop trying to help her get these transmissions."

James bit his lip harder. *What does this mean to you?*

Ryann looked up and met his eyes. "I just want to be good to her. While I can," she said quietly.

James nodded and got up. He walked over to the pile of boxes he and Ryann had tucked in the corner of the kitchen behind a tarp. He flung the tarp off, grabbed a butter knife off the counter, and began cutting the seals.

The boxes had been sitting there since the accident. Untouched for years. Ryann had gathered their parents' things together intending to put them into storage or throw them away, but days became weeks and then weeks turned into months, and there they sat.

James seemed too upset to be bothered with handling things gently. He rifled through their mother's research papers, tossing some of them on the ground. He kept opening boxes and discarding items haphazardly when they didn't yield what he was searching for. Their mom's ID badge clattered onto the kitchen floor, but he didn't even stop to pick it up.

Finally, his fingers closed around a small brown address book.

James crossed the room and stood beside Ryann's chair. He flipped through the address book, folded it open, handed it to her, and pointed to a name. Then he leaned down and kissed her tenderly on the forehead.

Another way. Use it wisely.

He picked up Charlie, went into his room, and closed the door.

This letter is intended for Mr. Jiro Takanari who worked in the Engineering and Safety Center at NASA with Dr. Gillie Bird. If he is no longer in this position, please remit this back to sender or forward to his last known address.

Hi Mr. Takanari,

I don't know if you remember me, but I'm Dr. Gillie's daughter, Ryann. I hope you are doing well.

I am sorry for contacting you out of the blue like this but I feel like you may be able to help me with something. Recently I became acquaintances with a girl named Alexandria Macallough. You may know her as The Uninaut's Daughter. She has spent a lot of time and effort trying to receive messages from her mom and only has access to basic materials like radio scanners. SCOUT hasn't given her access to any information and she really deserves to have at least something. My mom mentioned that you had been monitoring this mission, but I don't know how much information you were able to get. It was also a very long time ago, and I understand if it's no longer relevant to what you're working on now.

I just wanted to reach out and find out if you have any resources, or can point me in the direction of someone who does.

I know we haven't ever spoken, but I remember you being good friends with my mom. I hope that's enough for you to at least consider it.

As you may know, I am the sole provider for my brother, James, and we are caring for a one-year-old boy. We have been attending school, but winter break just started and I would really like to use the free time to work on this.

Thank you for your consideration,
Ryann Bird

Dear Ryann Bird,

There are few things left in this world that could have surprised me more than receiving this letter. I remember your mother fondly and am pleased to hear that you and your brother are doing well.

I was unaware that Mr. Macallough moved to the area. However, I am very surprised that SCOUT has withheld data from the next of kin of their cohort. I do not believe that they would do so unless there were some extenuating circumstances. I am sure you will be able to explain in more detail at a later date.

It is very interesting to hear that you have been following the first *Odyssey* mission. NASA is a direct competitor with SCOUT but our research division has been following the mission as well. I'm certain that you've heard all the recordings Mr. Macallough has and I am limited by what I am authorized to share with the public, but if you are interested we have intercepted a full gallery of all the images sent back from the ship.

I would be happy to see you and your brother(s?) during your winter break.

Let me know when you are available to come by.

I am looking forward to making your acquaintance again after all this time and it gives me great joy to see you following in your mother's footsteps in regards to your interest in space exploration.

Jiro Takanari

Mr. Takanari,

Thank you so much! I didn't expect to get a response!

I wanted to ask you something about the *Odyssey* archive. Is there any way that me and some of my friends can come as well to see what you have from it? Mr. Macallough doesn't have more than ten or so recordings and no pictures at all. Until recently, they were using some basic radio equipment to record what they can, and only when either of them are awake and available to monitor for messages.

It would mean the world to my friend Alexandria if she could get to hear more than she's had access to.

If it's too much, I understand.

Thank you for your time,
Ryann Bird

Dear Ryann,

As this is a military facility, the center is not open to the public. Additionally, the research lab dedicated to monitoring and archiving data from the mission is an internal department. I will only be able to get visitors' rights for you and your siblings as next of kin of former staff. Additionally, you will be unable to take or record anything while you are visiting.

I hope you understand.

Jiro Takanari

Mr. Takanari,

I do, thank you.

Ryann Bird

4 DAYS

The Bird siblings rode nearly an hour to the NASA base on the back of Ryann's bike. Ryann was wearing the only non-black clothing she owned—a gray T-shirt and blue jeans. She'd combed her short hair and pulled it into a tight bun. James watched her with curious dark eyes as she ran around getting ready. He'd opted to arrive as he was. This wasn't an important day for him.

When they pulled up to the front gate, they showed their IDs to the armed guard and were fingerprinted before they were allowed into the parking lot.

Standing at the front gate was a tall elderly man with his hands clasped behind his back, waiting for them.

Ryann parked as close to the gate as she could.

Mr. Takanari watched them calmly as they approached, Ryann nervous with her helmet tucked under her arm, James cold and curious as he'd been that entire morning.

"You're taller than when I last saw you," Mr. Takanari said, his eyes crinkling warmly. "You both look so much like Gillie."

"Hi," Ryann said bashfully. Mr. Takanari glanced over her shoulder at James. To Ryann's surprise, James signed hello and then motioned to his ear, shrugging.

"I see. I am sorry," Mr. Takanari said, clearly assuming that James lost his hearing in the accident that claimed their parents. Ryann was scandalized.

"Please follow me. I'm sure you're both excited," he said finally, and he began making his way through the security gate.

As soon as Mr. Takanari's back was turned, Ryann whipped around to glare at James.

"You're not deaf," she mouthed. "That's rude."

James looked at her dryly. "Easier," he mouthed back, then snapped twice and pointed. Mr. Takanari was getting farther away from them so Ryann jogged to keep up.

10 MINUTES

They went through two sets of metal detectors and had their belongings tagged and stored before they were allowed in. James looked irritated at having to relinquish his phone, but since he'd lied about knowing sign language to Mr. Takanari, he just had to deal with it.

Ryann was privately pleased that she didn't have to carry her helmet the whole time, but James's irritation put a damper on that. She squeezed his shoulder and nodded at him sympathetically. They followed Mr. Takanari down the hall to a set of elevators.

"The last time we met, you were here working on a diorama. Did you ever manage to finish it?" Mr. Takanari asked kindly.

"Eventually." Ryann smiled. She had been working on a Science Fair project freshman year of high school and had taken a field trip to her mom's office to finish it.

"That's good to hear," Mr. Takanari said. "You always seemed so interested in your mother's work. I was more than a little concerned about what had happened to you after the accident. You know, in that way where you know that you will never know, of course. But you always were at the very back of my mind."

"Oh. Thank you."

They left the elevators and followed Mr. Takanari down a long hallway, past a few glass-walled offices filled with people. The closer they got to her mother's former office, the more familiar everything looked—the posters on the wall and even some of the faces passing. No one stopped them or said hello, but it was nice all the same.

"We remodeled a bit but things should look pretty much the same," Mr. Takanari said over his shoulder.

"They do," Ryann said quietly.

"This way." Mr. Takanari led them down a quiet corridor and through a series of open offices into a dark room with a screen that was so wide it nearly touched both walls. He spread his fingers across it and moved icons around, pulling up digital files and arranging them into a slideshow and audio queue.

"I was able to make a little presentation before you came," Mr. Takanari said. "We have pictures from the launch day all the way up to last week when they reached Haumea's orbit."

"You don't have any audio files, though," Ryann said.

Mr. Takanari looked over his shoulder. "It is not a question of whether we have them. We do. It is a question of whether we are allowed to show them to the public. We are not. You see, this information does not belong to us. We are able to receive it because there is no way for SCOUT to prevent that. However, we do not own it and therefore we cannot distribute it the way we usually do. This information is not in the public domain, it belongs to SCOUT, and it can only be given out by SCOUT. The images, however, are under a different sort of federal regulation license and are in the public domain, unlike research data or personal transmissions, so luckily I am able to share them with you."

He clicked a few tabs on the screen, then clapped the lights off.

THE UNINAUTS

The first pictures were of the Uninauts hanging out with one another. The girls looked incredibly young and very excited, but all fifteen of them had the same incredibly tense look in their eyes. Alexandria's mom looked strikingly similar to Alexandria; the jut of her chin and the tightness of her jaw were the same. James glanced over at Ryann, his eyebrows knit in confusion.

"They were only seventeen or eighteen. About your age," Mr. Takanari said, stroking his chin. "Very brave, all of them."

The images shifted to launch photos and eventually to snaps of the Earth pulling away from them. Next, there was the moon and a few more silly pictures of the Uninauts, but as they flew past Mars's orbit, the photographs took on a significantly more academic feel. More images of different angles, close-ups and zoomed-in parts of Jupiter.

James's hand tightened in Ryann's grip as he watched. She understood. He didn't really care for science, he liked literature and history. This was probably the first time he'd seen pictures like these.

As they neared Pluto's orbit, the images shifted to zoomed-in pictures of the stars and far away images of the sun. There were a few more images of the Uninauts peppered in, but fewer than before. They all looked much more serious and the pictures were more like portraits than candids. It gave Ryann an eerie feeling. Like they were trying to document themselves in the same way as they were documenting the stars.

Mr. Takanari watched Ryann and James watch the presentation until it ended, and then he turned on the light.

"You both look like you could use a cup of tea," he said. James was looking hard at the ground, his ears lightly pink. He let go of Ryann's hand.

"Yes," Ryann's voice cracked. "Yes, thank you."

35 MINUTES

The cafeteria was surprisingly sparsely populated. Most of the staff seemed to be buying lunch and taking it with them instead of sitting at any of the tables.

Mr. Takanari left them at a table by the window and went to get their drinks. Ryann couldn't see anything but waving grass and fields of corn as far as her vision stretched. James had shaken off the melancholy he'd had and was doing the face he made when he was trying to see the best in something.

Ryann reached over and covered his hand with hers. He startled, but then he curled his palm over so they were holding hands again.

Mr. Takanari came back and placed three steaming cups of black tea on the table. He pushed a small piece of chocolate cake toward each of them and sat down. "How did you like the slideshow?"

Ryann couldn't quite find words to describe it.

Mr. Takanari didn't look surprised. "How much do you know about the mission?"

"I did a project on it, then Alexandria told me about it. I know as much as I could find out myself, I guess."

"I see," Mr. Takanari said. "Did your mother talk to you about it?"

"A bit, but I can't remember that much," Ryann admitted.

"When we first met, I was sure you would find yourself working here someday," Mr. Takanari said. "You were always running around asking questions and getting into things, and everybody used to tell your mom to stop complaining about it 'because she had a little scientist on her hands.' All she wanted was for you to sit down and read a book like James. What happened?"

Ryann shifted uncomfortably, but then she saw the grin tucked into the side of James's mouth and it made her feel a bit lighter.

"I'm still interested," she replied. "But I'm busy these days. I have a lot of responsibilities and I don't have the time to focus on anything that isn't a sure thing."

Mr. Takanari frowned.

"I'm sorry if that's disappointing to hear," Ryann said.

"I see. Well. If you're interested, I can tell you a bit about what happened, so you have something to take back to your friend."

"That's . . . thank you."

Mr. Takanari nodded and sat back in his chair, wrapping his large wrinkled hands around his cup. "Your mother supported the idea at first. They were picking people from all over the world and she said something very beautiful about it, if I remember correctly. She said, 'Diversity is a flower that blooms with greater beauty and greater strength each time it is cross-pollinated.' And I believe she was right."

THE LEGEND

"The issue wasn't the mission, or anything like that. It was more about the backlash," Mr. Takanari continued.

"Before NASA was absorbed by the U.S. military, it was an incredibly difficult time politically. Our military had the largest budget in the world and we had nothing. The work we did was of interest for international trade agreements, and we found ourselves in a good position to bargain for a merger.

"We received an incredible amount of funding and resources, and in exchange we tarnished our social positioning within the global scientific community. We 'sold out' as it was. As you can see, the lasting effects of that barely scratched our day-to-day operations—we just have more security and better coffee—but back then it was absolutely scandalous." Mr. Takanari shook his head on that last word, like it pained him to say it. Then he continued.

"As an effect of this, SCOUT arose from our ashes. They were a brand-new company with a hotshot young founder who was radically invested in rebranding space exploration as a bohemian, stateless activity for the betterment of all mankind.

"He was personable and he made good, reasonable points and he really energized people about the idea of becoming pioneers. His global interest made him popular in the international scientific community and he received an incredible amount of support—both socially and financially."

Mr. Takanari stopped to take a few sips of his tea, then cleared his throat hard.

"It was a disaster from the beginning. No one could get much information from them about their company and how they were doing. SCOUT was very shiny on the outside but intensely private—and they had a right to be. They were privately owned, unlike NASA, where we share everything, like you really should. Everything about SCOUT was dramatically different from all other space exploration programs, but they were so confident, that people sort of nodded and accepted it.

"Even the launch was shiny, and we were all so terribly impressed that he'd managed to pull the whole thing off. But when the news broke about . . . your unfortunate friend and her . . . incredibly unfortunate mother, it didn't surprise much of anyone here. Of course it surprised everyone outside, but here in this office, in this community, it just seemed almost right. Something had to go wrong, it always does with space travel. At least it was this and not an explosion."

James glanced at Ryann curiously, but she shook her head.

"Your mother was incredibly upset. But there wasn't anything anyone could do. You can't barge into SCOUT's office and demand they drag their own rockets down from the sky." Mr. Takanari waved his hand angrily. "We did try to petition that they be shut down, but that never went anywhere. You tell your friend that we did try."

Ryann nodded. "What happened next?"

Mr. Takanari finished his tea and pushed the cup toward the middle of the table. "Hmm. After the petition went nowhere, we all appealed to the United Nations to draw up a series of accords that governed space exploration companies, requiring that certain information be made available within the international scientific community and additional safety and ethical measures must be decided upon by an international ethics committee. It was not the best outcome, but it was an outcome that improved things for the future. Your mother was very proud of it."

"Every time I hear about this, I learn something new," Ryann said as she looked into her cup.

Mr. Takanari smiled. "Every story has a hundred million perspectives. There is always something new in each of them. What really matters is the full picture when all the pieces are put together. In history, sometimes you can never find them all. But that is life, isn't it?"

2 HOURS AND 17 MINUTES

James held Ryann extra tight on their way home. He had that dark, curious look in his eyes again and didn't respond to any of Ryann's questions until they were outside their trailer.

He pulled the helmet off his head and typed quickly. *Does Alexandria know about the loneliness?*

Ryann scrunched up her nose. "Of what?"

Of space. Of all this.

Ryann stared at the screen for a while. "Yeah," she said finally. "Alexandria does."

James frowned and then typed for a long time. *You can go to SCOUT and try to get her messages. But be careful. We love you.*

Ryann read the message and reached out for a hug, but James turned quickly and went to go retrieve Charlie from the neighbor's house.

Ryann let her arms fall gently to her sides.

JANUARY

Blake swung by the trailer park to pick Ryann up, then they all headed over state lines. Ryann got into the passenger's seat, nodding a hello to Alexandria in the back seat. All of them were too anxious to talk.

Tomas followed behind them.

When they were nearly there, Tomas peeled off their tail and headed somewhere nearby to wait.

Ryann glanced over at Blake. His eyes followed Tomas until he slipped from sight, then they returned to the road.

The SCOUT building was large and white, with only two obvious entrance points. There were a few cars left in the parking lot, so they were sure almost everyone had gone home.

"Are you ready?" Alexandria asked.

Blake took a deep breath. Then he rolled his window down and waved Alexandria's dad's ID at the scanner.

The light at the end of the gate turned green. Blake let out the breath he'd been holding and pulled forward past the attendant and into the parking lot.

Blake pulled over to the side of the building, next to the Dumpsters, and parked.

Ryann and Alexandria got out of the car. Alexandria

pulled a ski mask down over her face and pulled on her gloves. Blake popped the trunk so Ryann could grab their bookbags.

"Don't tell the others I asked, but are you sure you want to go through with this?" Blake said. He eyed them both warily. "The only people here are us. We could just . . . I wouldn't tell anyone if you decided to cut your losses."

Alexandria glanced at Ryann, but Ryann tapped the roof of the car resolutely. "Keep the engine running in case we need a quick getaway," she told Blake. "If you see the cops, feel free to drive off. We won't need a ride if they show up."

"Okay. Good luck." Blake rolled up the window.

4 MINUTES

The front door was locked and didn't respond to the key card. Two other side doors also failed to let them in. But a fire door near the rear opened easily and didn't seem to have a functioning alarm.

Ryann motioned for Alexandria to follow her down a hallway to the front desk, which was empty. She opened the desk drawers and rummaged around inside.

"What are you looking for?" Alexandria whispered.

"The network password." Ryann said. "Everyone gets paperwork when they start working somewhere, and it usually has information like that. If we're lucky, they kept it . . ." She closed one drawer and opened another. "Plus, it's the front desk. Chances are the admin that works here keeps stuff like that on file in case visitors ask."

Alexandria sat down on the floor near the wall and plugged in her laptop.

Ryann opened a folder and began flipping through the contents. She stopped. "Really?"

Alexandria looked up, concerned. "What?"

Ryann shoved the folder back into the desk. "The password is SCOUT1234. The guest one is SCOUTGUEST1234."

Alexandria smirked. "That's so . . ."

"Simplistic? Easily hackable? Dumb as hell? All the above."

"All the above. But it worked. We're in."

Ryann sat down next to Alexandria and scooted close so she could look over her shoulder.

The SCOUT website was plain and white, not particularly aesthetically appealing. Alexandria's dad's email account seemed to still be active so Alexandria began drafting a message. Ryann took out Ahmed's tablet and logged in as well. She started looking for access points that could potentially lead to records.

She was so focused on that, she didn't hear anything until a flashlight beam lit them both.

"Stand up with your hands in view."

Alexandria startled so hard she dropped her laptop. The cord yanked out of the wall and the screen went black as it slammed to the ground.

Ryann gently put Ahmed's tablet on the floor and climbed to her feet, squinting into the light.

43 SECONDS

The flashlight lowered just enough that Ryann could see that it was the guard from the front gate. He was an older man and he looked more confused than angry.

"We're not stealing anything!" Alexandria blurted.

"You're just kids ... What are you doing in here?" he asked. "You can't be in here after hours."

"We'll go right now," Ryann said. They could probably still access the Internet if they stayed close to the building now that they were logged in.

"I can't let you do that, I'm afraid. All visitors need to be photographed and have their identification processed. Gather your things, we have to go down to the security office ... and don't try to run or anything." He eyed them suspiciously. "We have cameras and the doors are locked."

Alexandria scrambled her things together and Ryann gently put Ahmed's tablet back in her bookbag.

"How did you get in here?" the old man continued as he watched them. "There's nothing around worth stealing that you could carry out in your hands. I had to do a double take on the security monitors when you all drove by. Where'd you get an ID?"

"It's my dad's," Alexandria said miserably.

The old man began walking down the hallway and gestured for them to follow. "Well," he said over his shoulder, "technically, since I let you in, it isn't breaking and entering in the traditional sense. We might have to have a talk about identity theft, but so long as the cameras didn't catch you destroying property, we might not have to get the police involved."

Alexandria opened her mouth to say something but Ryann shook her head.

2 MINUTES

They rode the elevator with him in uncomfortable silence. When they reached the basement, he gestured for them to go out in front of him. "First door on your right. Grab a seat in front of the large desk and look straight at the black square on the wall."

He sat down behind the desk and fiddled with the keyboard for a bit.

"Pictures done. You got any ID on you?" he asked. "I'm going to need that ID card you have as well. Your dad a current employee?"

"No," Alexandria said.

Ryann handed over her driver's license, Alexandria's state ID, and Alexandria's father's ID card.

The security officer took photos of their IDs and then pushed them to the edge of the desk.

"You know, my son used to do things like this. Get into trouble here and there," he said. "Always hoped he would grow out of it."

He entered Alexandria's father's ID card into a small slit on the computer monitor and pulled up security footage from inside the building and skimmed through it. Alexandria looked over at Ryann anxiously, but Ryann shook her head. If she'd learned anything about being in trouble, it was that the less you said the better. They hadn't broken anything, stolen anything, or done anything but log in to the network. From the way things looked like they were going, they might just get a slap on the wrist and be kicked out.

It would suck that they didn't get what they came for, but it was easier to go home knowing they tried.

Suddenly the security officer made an interesting face. He did a double take at Alexandria, then he picked up the phone and dialed an extension.

"Hello, this is John. Glad you're still in the office. I have a bit of a situation and I think you might want to come down here and see . . . No, nothing's broken, it's more of a . . . yeah. I'll forward it over. Yeah, it's no problem and thank you, I do try. See you in a bit."

Alexandria started getting up, but the security officer pointed a finger at her and sternly said, "Sit. Don't make things worse."

20 MINUTES

They sat in silence for what felt like ages. Alexandria stared at the floor. The security guard kept looking over at them, but he didn't say anything else. He seemed just as anxious as they were.

The elevator dinged down the hall and they both looked up.

A man rounded the corner and swiped his ID to open the door. He looked to be in his late forties, and he was very neatly dressed in an expensive black sweater and slacks. He had brown hair with a touch of gray at the temples and horn-rimmed glasses. He strode into the room, nodding hello at the guard.

The security guard had his arms folded and a tight look on his face. He gestured over to Ryann and Alexandria. All at once, Ryann realized that the look on the security guard's face wasn't for them, it was for this man.

The man turned around and went completely ashen.

He stared at them for a moment, then covered his mouth and looked at the ground.

The air was so still that Ryann could hear the camera on the wall quietly whining and the buzz of the ID scanner on the other side of the door.

The man dropped his hand from his mouth and crossed his arms tightly in front of himself. His eyes wandered over

Ryann contemplatively for a moment, then shifted to Alexandria, who was staring back at him, her cheeks growing red with fury.

The man opened his mouth, then closed it again and swallowed. He tried again. "Alexandria."

Her name tore itself out of him like it was pulled. It was rough, cracking in the middle.

"You're—" he continued, then stopped himself. He blinked rapidly, then turned to Ryann and stuck out a hand to be shook. "Roland Mark," he said. "SCOUT founder and CEO. It's . . . a pleasure . . . ," he trailed off.

"Ryann Bird," Ryann replied, glancing over at Alexandria quickly as she shook Roland's hand.

He offered a hand to Alexandria, who predictably did not take it. Roland let his arm fall gently to his side.

3 SECONDS

Roland visibly composed himself, glancing over his shoulder at the security guard. "You can go. We don't need to get the police involved. Thank you for calling me downstairs."

The security guard eyed Roland as he stood and adjusted his belt. Then he nodded to Ryann and Alexandria. "It's good to see you again, kid," he said, and walked out the door.

Roland jerked as if he'd been shook.

After a moment of silence, he sat down on the floor in front of them, cross-legged like a child.

"John has been here since the beginning," he explained, taking off his glasses and rubbing his eyes. "He held you on your first day."

Alexandria reached forward and slapped him with astonishing speed.

Roland's hair fell over his face and he took another moment to compose himself. Then he looked back up at Alexandria from his place on the ground. Ryann watched, remembering the night Alexandria had thrown a rock at her, and her heart beat fiercely with pride.

1 MINUTE AND 12 SECONDS

"It's not every day," Roland began, "that you get to stare your failures in the face and see how they've grown and changed." He swallowed and then said very gently, "Alexandria Macallough, I am so, *so* sorry."

Alexandria stood up quickly. "You don't get to say that. You don't get to—"

"I was thirty-one years old," Roland continued quietly. "I had just gotten my PhD, I hadn't even been out of school for more than a year. SCOUT was . . . just a project I was working on. I never thought it would go anywhere. I hoped, of course, but so many start-up companies fail and I was ready for that failure. I expected it. When the opportunity came for investment, I just went out there and gave it my best shot. I was so nervous, and when they gave me the money I was even more terrified."

Roland's eyes were glued to the floor in front of them as he spoke. Alexandria stared down at him, luminous with fury.

"I wanted everything to be perfect," he said. "I cared a lot about the mission, I cared a lot about the people. I was good to my staff and I was good to my investors, and when we sought out the first cohort, we spent a whole year looking for recruits. Your mom, Eferhilde—"

"Don't say her name," Alexandria spat.

"She," Roland corrected. "She was kind and smart and empathetic. She didn't know until training was nearly half over. There wasn't time to look into any backups. I . . . If I had been more vigilant, I would have prepared for any of them to drop out, but I wasn't. Without her, they . . . Anyway. She had a meeting with medical staff and then a meeting with me. She wanted . . ."

Roland fell silent.

"Tell the whole truth," Ryann said.

Alexandria's hand balled into a fist on her thigh.

"She . . . wanted to tell your father, Raleigh Macallough—who was an undergrad intern at the time—immediately," Roland admitted, "but I coerced her into signing an NDA and persuaded her to wait. Just one more month, just one more week, just one more day, until it was too late. The PR would have been awful if it were announced to the public at six months. Worse if we announced it right before she left.

"The time was just never right . . . for me. Nor for her. For *us*, and I'll never forgive myself for that. We . . . kept you for those couple of months before she left while we were making a decision about what to do. I never went down to medical to visit you because I was panicking and not sleeping over it, and I was so angry that it had happened in the first place.

"I was angry back then, but I think I was also just guilty. I couldn't handle looking at you lying there, so small, while understanding that what happened with you would be my fault," he said quietly.

"I held you just once. John passed you into my arms himself. He wanted me to know the weight of my cowardice, he wanted my greed to have a face. He's still angry, even now. When . . . When I held my own daughter years later, I . . ." A tear streaked down his face. "I understood."

Alexandria sat back. She glanced at Ryann quickly, then refocused on Roland, who hadn't made eye contact with either of them since he began.

"We . . . I asked them to take you to your father's house," he said. "To just give you to him, so I could wash my hands of the whole thing and refocus my energy on monitoring the lives of the Uninauts and the success of the mission. But that was wrong. I should have taken responsibility for that.

"Raleigh's family sued and we settled out of court, but that tiny blip was enough on the radar of our competitors, and news of your circumstances leaked until it was wildly out of control."

Roland closed his eyes, covered them with his hand, and continued, "Your . . . young father showed up at our offices and demanded to be taken to see me. When we were finally alone, he threatened to kill me. He said that he hoped that I was crushed under the weight of my own ambition. We argued about it and eventually it was decided that he was a danger to both myself and the company, so we drew up safety measures to protect ourselves from him and to protect him from the consequences of his own anger. We've been watching him and eventually you, too, ever since."

Roland finally looked up.

"I have spent the past almost twenty years working to reform this company around the lessons I learned from that moment. But I still wasn't prepared to have you standing in front of me like this."

Alexandria's mouth turned sharply down, and she said nothing for a long time.

"You are doing it again. This mission. Why?" Ryann asked.

Roland took a deep breath and wiped his face. "The technology is better, our ships are faster. The first mission was well funded, but there were some medical complications. We have spent the past twenty years working to make this time better and we will. People don't want to know about the price of things like this. They want the glamour of space and the pretty pictures and the romanticism—"

"They don't want the danger, and the darkness and loneliness," Alexandria interrupted softly. "They want the heat and the light, but they don't want radiation."

Roland closed his mouth and looked at Alexandria with indescribable pain and indescribable fondness.

"The stars have weight," Alexandria finished. "And my little life wasn't heavy enough to outweigh your want of it."

Roland nodded. "Yes," he said roughly. "At that time, yes."

4 MINUTES

Ryann eyed the locked door, then turned back to Roland.

"What happens now?" she asked.

Roland swallowed hard and cleared his throat. He blinked rapidly and sat up straighter. "I want to offer you an opportunity," he said.

Alexandria looked up, her eyes bright with unshed, angry tears. "Don't offer anything you can't afford to give," she said furiously.

"I am offering . . . ," Roland said, "what I *owe*, Alexandria Macallough. There is a space on this ship that is meant for an everyman. We were going to host a contest for it, let people apply. The idea behind it was that we wanted someone who could represent the average person. The only thing it would require is pilot training and a few basic tests—things anyone suited for space travel can pass without being a genius or wunderkind."

He pulled out his phone and started typing into it. "We were going to do the campaign for it next month, but I'm postponing it until—"

"Give me a week," Alexandria interrupted.

"But this is what you told me you wanted in October—" Ryann blurted frantically.

"A week," Alexandria said resolutely. "And I will let you know."

Roland nodded.

Alexandria stood and looked down at him, drowning him in the silhouette of her shadow.

"I forgive you," she said.

He let out a breath that it seemed he had been holding since he arrived. Then he dug in his pocket and pulled out a flash drive.

"Here. When he called me downstairs, I thought it was Raleigh. I . . . owe him this. The audio files and the transcripts. Please make sure he gets them."

He gently placed those years in the softness of Alexandria's palm.

6 MINUTES AND 4 SECONDS

They walked out into the hallway. Alexandria was shaking terribly. She dropped her flashlight and then bent down to pick it up but dropped it again. She covered her eyes and sobbed.

Ryann picked up the flashlight and helped Alexandria to her feet.

"We'll figure this out," Ryann said. "But we need to get out of here."

Alexandria nodded. She didn't let go.

They walked quickly to the exit, picking up the pace until they were running hand in hand to the doors.

3 MINUTES AND 49 SECONDS

They burst outside. Tomas and Blake were sitting in Blake's car waiting for them. At the looks on Ryann's and Alexandria's faces, Blake immediately went pale. He opened the door and got out.

"Are you okay?" he asked frantically.

Alexandria burst into tears, unable to handle responding to that. Tomas hopped out of the passenger seat, ran around the car, and pulled Alexandria into the back with him.

"We met the CEO and talked to him for a while," Ryann said. "I'll tell you about it later, but we need to go."

Blake nodded resolutely. He hopped back into the car and they screeched off into the night.

56 MINUTES

Alexandria cried herself to sleep in the back of Blake's car. Tomas switched vehicles and began following them to the hotel Shannon had booked.

Ryann turned the flash drive over and over in her hand. Blake glanced over at it but said nothing.

Shannon had booked Blake and Tomas a room separate from Ryann and Alexandria, but Tomas insisted on them all sharing. He was horrified to silence as Ryann sat across from him on the hotel bed and described what had happened.

Blake, who normally would have been incredibly irritated by having to share a bed with Tomas, took it in stride wordlessly. He shucked his jeans and sweater and lay down next to Tomas. He didn't move away when Tomas curled into him. He just stared at the ceiling blankly.

Ryann sat on the edge of her bed and looked through the wall, disassociating a bit. She could hear Alexandria sniffling out on the balcony. As soon as they had gotten in the room Alexandria'd thrown all her gear in the corner, slammed the glass doors behind her, and been out there for nearly an hour.

Ryann understood.

"What are we telling the others?" Blake asked suddenly.

Ryann turned to him. Tomas was curled into his shoulders, completely asleep, while Blake gently brushed his fingers through the other boy's hair.

"It's not our story to tell," Ryann said. "I'll ask Alexandria, but whatever she wants is what we'll do." She leaned over and turned off the bedside lamp, plunging the room into darkness.

"Okay," Blake agreed. "What are you going to do about that?" He nodded to the balcony.

Ryann glanced at Alexandria's silhouette through the curtains.

"She doesn't respond to being comforted," Ryann said. "She burns off her anger."

Blake nodded and closed his eyes.

3 HOURS

Ryann woke up with a start. It was still dark outside. She glanced at the clock on the nightstand and saw that it was barely one a.m.

Alexandria sat on the bed next to her. She took a drag from her cigarette, then tapped the ash into the tray on the bedside table and exhaled through her teeth.

Ryann sat up. Alexandria offered her the cigarette and Ryann took it, placing her lips where Alexandria's had been.

"It's difficult to be angry for so long," Alexandria said. "Then to look your monster in the face, and it's just some asshole who has had more years to learn what it means to be sorry than you've had to be mad." She took the cigarette back.

"I'm sorry," Ryann said, her voice still rough from sleep.

Alexandria shook her head. "Don't . . . don't say that. I do fully understand why my dad hated them now, at least. I don't think there's anything Roland could have said that would have had an impact on him in any way. But the perspective is . . . I don't know."

Ryann shifted closer and plucked the cigarette out of Alexandria's hand and took another breath of ash. "Blake wants to know if we're going to tell the others?"

"Why wouldn't we? They helped and they deserve to be a part of things," Alexandria said scathingly.

"*I know*," Ryann said soothingly. "I know. He's just trying to care about us all in the only way he can."

Alexandria looked over at Tomas and Blake. "Are they a thing now?"

Ryann laughed mirthlessly. "I don't think so. But I've been wondering that for years."

4 HOURS AND 10 MINUTES

Ryann woke up again. This time it was near dawn and the room was lit in shades of pink and gold. She looked over to find Alexandria still awake.

"Did you stay up the whole night?" Ryann whispered.

Alexandria didn't move. Instead she said, "You pinkie promised me something and I want to cash in on that."

Ryann turned over on her side so she could see Alexandria properly. "What do you want?"

"Remember when we were walking in the woods and you told everyone why you were helping me?" Alexandria asked.

"Yeah, I—"

"When you said that you wished you could . . . but that you had responsibilities and had to let your dreams go?" Alexandria interrupted.

Ryann frowned. "I'm not helping you because of that anymore. I did this because you deserve to have someone on your side. And because . . ." The words caught in her throat.

Alexandria waited for them, then she laughed dryly, the way she did when something upset her and the only way to deal with it was to laugh at her own misfortune.

Ryann, always reckless this close to sleep, reached across the sheets and picked up Alexandria's hand. Alexandria's eyes went dark. She caught Ryann's jaw in her palm, holding it fast.

Instantly, Ryann was fully awake, her heart slamming in her chest as Alexandria studied her. The last time Alexandria had looked at her like this, it was in the silence of Shannon's bedroom, with her knees between Ryann's thighs.

Alexandria moved her thumb over Ryann's chin and settled it against the fullest part of Ryann's bottom lip, then pressed until Ryann's mouth fell gently open.

The sun from the balcony doors lit Alexandria's eyelashes white and shot her brown eyes through with light.

"I want you to go," Alexandria whispered. "Take my place. I want you to be selfish for the first time in your life, Ryann Bird. I'll carry your weight. You're worth the price."

Ryann's mouth watered with the need to touch the tip of her tongue to Alexandria's thumb—to bite and lick. But before she could, Alexandria took her hand away and held out her pinkie. The rush of cold air on Ryann's face nearly made her lean up to recapture it.

Alexandria's eyes tracked the motion hungrily, but she said nothing.

She waited until Ryann reached her sleep-warm hand from under the blankets and locked their pinkies together.

7 MINUTES

Tomas and Blake woke up soon after. Tomas looked shocked at Blake's arms around him and started trying to wriggle out from underneath without waking him up.

Blake buried his face in Tomas's neck as he slowly regained consciousness, but pulled away immediately when his eyes opened. Tomas turned around to face him.

Blake blinked up at Tomas sleepily, then put up his fist. Tomas fist-bumped it, seemingly resolving whatever Ryann and Alexandria had just witnessed.

Alexandria still eyed them contemplatively as she got dressed.

Tomas lumbered sleepily over and hugged Alexandria— who was a little more than shocked that he was touching her. Tomas also curled into Ryann as well, hugging her for a suspiciously long time, and then he disappeared into the bathroom.

Blake shoved his legs through his jeans, then quickly put on his sweater and jacket. "Meet me outside when you're ready."

29 MINUTES

The ride back was calmer and less tense than the ride up.

Ryann received a text forwarded from Alexandria, giving her a time she should arrive, a room number, and instructions for check-in at SCOUT's headquarters. Roland must have sent it to Alexandria last night.

Her chest tightened as she looked at it. Alexandria, who could see Ryann's screen from the back seat, gripped Ryann's shoulder and the tension drifted away beneath her fingers.

3 HOURS AND 49 SECONDS

Ahmed was pacing outside the warehouse when they pulled in around noon.

Shannon and James were waiting inside. The fire pit was lit and Shannon was typing feverishly into her laptop.

"Did you get it?" Ahmed said, rushing to Ryann's side. "You're not in jail, so that's a good sign at least."

"We did get it," Ryann said.

"Can I borrow your laptop?" Tomas asked as he sat on the rug.

"Yeah." Ahmed pushed Shannon's laptop to Alexandria, who stuck the flash drive in.

"What happened?" Shannon asked.

"I met Roland," Alexandria said. "He . . . was staying late in the office and came down to intercept us after we were caught by security. He had a breakdown and told me about his involvement in the circumstances of my birth." Alexandria put her bookbag on the floor and settled into the silence. "He apologized, and it was a terrible and pathetic thing. I forgave him because he was honest."

"Oh my God," Ahmed breathed.

"What happened next?" Shannon said.

Ryann glanced quickly at Alexandria, who gazed back at

her meaningfully. "It was . . . surreal," Ryann said. "He also gave us the sound files we were looking for and offered us a proposition."

Ryann stopped and looked at James.

James typed something rapidly and showed it to Shannon.

"What kind of proposition?" Shannon said, reading his text out loud.

Ryann felt Alexandria staring at her. She opened her mouth to explain but Tomas cut her off. "He asked if Alexandria wanted to be recruited for the next cohort. He offered the opportunity to go to space on their next mission as an apology for all the shit that he did to Alexandria's family." Tomas tossed a nearby stick into the bonfire and refused to make eye contact with the others.

"Then, later, Alexandria gave that opportunity to Ryann instead," Tomas said. "It would be stupid to refuse an offer like that," he continued, now staring at Ryann. "So don't even waste our time trying to convince us you aren't going to take it."

He looked over his shoulder directly into Ryann's eyes. "I heard you talking this morning," he said. "It's more assholish that you waited to tell everyone about something this important than for me to just tell them for you," he said bitterly.

Ryann jerked back as if struck. So that was why Tomas had hugged her for an unusually long time back at the hotel.

Blake folded his arms tightly in front of himself and scowled into the fire. Shannon and Ahmed both looked outraged at Tomas, and Ryann could see Shannon digging her nails into Ahmed's arm.

James stared at Ryann in horror for a second. Then he made a terrible noise, the first sound Ryann had heard him make since the accident, and it dropped her heart to the center of the Earth. She reached out for him, but he pushed past her and ran off into the woods.

Ryann leaped up and ran after him.

A MOMENT. A YEAR.

James was fast. Ryann had forgotten that.

He bobbed and weaved through the trees as Ryann scrambled after him.

"Stop!" she screamed, but he didn't listen. He just ran until Ryann couldn't see him anymore. She could hear the river nearby, churning in the distance, and her heart caught in her throat.

"Jamie!" she shrieked.

Ryann picked through the brambles until she found him, curled up at the base of a tree, sobbing into his arms.

Ryann hopped over a branch and slipped in some mud, then crashed into her little brother, folding him tightly into the circle of her arms. James cried desperately, clinging to Ryann's back.

"Jamie, Jamie, Jamie." Ryann rocked him back and forth.

"Pl—" James's voice cut off and his lips moved with the sound of hissing air.

"I hear you," Ryann said "I *hear* you. I wanted to talk to you first. I didn't think that Tomas would just—"

"I'll w—y—" James yelled in frustration, air hissing between the words.

"I'm sorry," Ryann said. "I won't go. I won't go."

James pushed Ryann off so he could stare into her face. He gripped her cheeks in both hands and pressed their foreheads together and sobbed.

After a moment, he pulled his phone out of his pocket and typed: *You deserve to. You've always deserved more than this.*

"I don't deserve anything that you don't get to share," Ryann said.

James laughed sharply through his tears and began typing again. *I don't mean it like that. I'm upset because I can't hold you back, because I want you to go but I didn't think it would be this soon.*

"I don't have to go. I would give this up for you." Ryann wiped James's face with her mittens.

James took a deep breath and threw his head up to look at the sky. *How many years would it take for you to resent me.*

"I would never resent you for this," Ryann promised. She instinctively raised her pinkie finger, but James batted it away.

Love is not about holding people where you want them. It is about doing what's best for them because you need them to be okay.

Charlie's mom, Adeline, taught me that. She knew we would do a better job with him than she could, so she gave him up. She taught me that before she left. I'm teaching you that now.

Go.

Don't forget us, but go.

Ryann nodded. She wiped James's face again, then pulled him close.

"You're nearly grown," Ryann said. "You're responsible and strong and smart. You're a good father and a good brother and a good friend. You will heal from this." She shook him once for emphasis.

James rested his head on her shoulder in despair, but he sniffed and took a few more deep breaths.

"I'll always be here." Ryann took his cold hands and blew on his knuckles.

I know.

28 MINUTES

When they got back to the warehouse, everyone was sitting in silence. Ahmed sat up quickly and pulled Ryann and James to sit next to him and Shannon.

"I'm not talking to you about this," Ahmed said harshly, holding fast to Ryann's arm. "This is a decision that I don't want the responsibility of having influenced—for better or worse."

Ryann held his gaze, then nodded, answering him. Ahmed squeezed her arm gently, then let her go.

"Are you okay?" Shannon asked James quietly. James nodded but wiped his eyes again, hard.

"Okay. So," Blake said, "we're going to play the audio files. They had them organized by activity and there was a folder just for family. The rest are official reports or text files, which apparently she sent more often."

He turned to the Bird siblings. "Are you sure you guys want to stay for this?"

Ryann turned to James. His eyes flickered over to Alexandria, who was sitting between Tomas and Blake, looking at the ground despondently.

Do it, he typed.

[fiddling with mic] Hello? Is . . . is this working right? I've never used one of—Hello? Oh, the red light—okay, well, hey, Raleigh. I hope things are going as well for you down there as they are for me up here . . .

The guys are so excited; I'm having trouble believing I'm even here. I keep pinching myself but the only thing that happens is I get more welts.

[laughter]

But, oh, you would love it up here. It's beautiful. It's . . . it's everything. I mean, we see pictures and videos back home, but it's nothing as good as the real thing. It's hard to even describe.

I wish you were here to see it.

I wish I could show it to you.

This is a grand adventure but I'd be lying if I said I didn't miss you already.

Anyway, I gotta go—Zhang Yong's up next and she has ten times the family to say hi to.

Anyway.

I love you to the moon and back. Tell the kiddo
I said hello.

Till next time.

Effie

Hey, Raleigh, it's me, Effie.

We had a bit of a scare—things got kind of rocky out here—but we got all patched up and everything seems to be going smoothly for now. I sent you back some pictures of the Earth and stuff from the ship; I hope they got to you safe and sound.

I hope you're doing all right. I . . . I hope a lot of things, you know? I'm glad to hear that Alex is doing all right. It's a bit sad to think that I won't get to see a lot of all the growing up stuff like walking and . . . I don't know, whatever the hell else babies do. But I'm pretty sure you've got that handled, you were always good at landing on your feet.

I know your ma probably still isn't too happy about . . . everything, but thankfully, unless she can learn to fly and breathe in a vacuum, she can't chase my sorry hide up here and kick my ass for leaving you with all that responsibility. And I am sorry. I really am. Tell her that for me.

Anyway.

I know you're probably wondering what we all

do up here, but it really isn't as interesting as you think. I mostly spend my limited free time reading. And I know you're rolling your eyes at that, but I like it more now than I did back at school.

We have these tablets with hundreds of thousands of stories on them—probably enough to last me until I die. There's this one that I finished the other day that I think you would like called *The Time Traveler's Wife* by . . . some lady I don't know. [rustling] It's on my bed, I uh . . . I don't have a head for names, but anyway. If I remember I'll tell you. It's real good though.

I have a couple of new friends. Zhang Yong's pretty swell—and way funnier than you'd assume. She's got that kind of dry humor where she keeps her face completely blank and says just about the craziest things you've heard in your whole life, and the combination of the face and the words makes it even funnier. Anyway, Zhang Yong went to school with Fimi for a year. I don't know if you remember her, but she's the girl from the Congo—real smart. But yeah, they kind of knew each other already and we got to talking and, well. At least I don't have to eat alone anymore.

This is getting kind of long, but I figured I owed you one since my first was so short.

Love you and love Alex and don't forget to tell your ma I'm sorry.

To the moon and back.

Effie

Hey, Raleigh,

Thank you for the birthday message! I didn't think you could get something like that out here without SCOUT's help, but you did it. [whistles] Roland must be heated. There ain't a minute that goes by that I'm not impressed with you.

Anyway, things are going . . . interestingly. Astrid and Gita hate each other now, so they're constantly fighting. Georgina—that English girl—has decided to give everyone the silent treatment because we made fun of how she says the word "been" like the word "bean." Then it caught on like a nickname and then her feelings got hurt and even though I didn't even start it AND I said sorry she still won't talk to me.

Maritza has a crush on Zhang now and she's being weird about it. She snuck her guitar on board and keeps playing songs whenever Zhang is nearby, and it's bad because I've known Zhang for a year and I'm pretty sure she doesn't like girls.

I mean anything could happen because we're trapped up here for eternity alone only with one another, but from the look on Zhang's face as I'm telling you this—*What? No, I'm not going to*—she doesn't even—*ugh, okay, fine.* Zhang says she wouldn't date Maritza if she was the last person on Earth—which, like I said, is strikingly similar to the scenario we currently find ourselves in. [sounds of struggle]

Ow! Quit hitting me, you know I'm right! You know I'm—we're not even on Earth so who cares what you do, with—Ow! Fimi! Fimi! Zhang keeps hi—

Hey, Raleigh, it's me, Eff.

Sorry about that last message. It's . . . well, you know how it is.

How's Alex? I wish I could hold her, you know? I miss her. We barely had any time. I got that picture you sent and I printed it out and stuck it above my bed. It helps and stuff, but . . .

I really miss you.

I miss the way your hair smells and that thing you do where you smile with one corner of your mouth higher than the other. I miss the way you pop your gum and the way you look when you get so wrapped up in studying you poke out your tongue a little. I miss walking to 7-Eleven at one a.m. and getting Slurpees and stargazing on the roof of my car. I miss sneaking in your window at night and sneaking out in the morning. I miss getting to talk to you when I'm sad or happy or upset and knowing you care what happens. I miss hearing your dreams and talking to you about what you wanna be when you grow up.

I miss thinking we could grow up together.

Because it didn't really occur to me until I was up here that this isn't growing up together, no matter how many messages we send or pictures I get. And we both know that when I get too far, your signal will be too weak and I'll get back nothing but silence from you, no matter how loud you'll be yellin'.

At the end of the day, I'm just up here and you're just down there and there's nothing we can do about it.

I . . . [sigh] I'm not trying to sound ungrateful. I'm still, I mean, the opportunity was one you just don't turn down . . . I just—Sometimes when everyone else has already gone to bed, I start feeling selfish and start thinking it would have been better to work at that steel warehouse and get to come home to you every day.

'Cause the stars are beautiful, but I'd give them up for good just to see your face.

Raleigh, it's me again.

You know, I left our planet to learn about the stars, but I think I'm learning more about people up here than I ever would back home.

The guys, they're all right, you know. Good, solid, smart of course. But before I was up here with them I never would have thought we'd all be so similar.

At least in the ways that matter.

They scraped us up from all over the world, you know, but up here, that doesn't mean a thing. You know Gita and Astrid grew up on a farm and didn't even start using the Internet until they were in high school? One of the Russian girls in engineering used to be so poor that she and her family would eat grass just to get by. Meanwhile, Maritza funded 15 percent of this mission out of her own pocket so she would get to go. She won't tell anyone how much it was because she says that money doesn't matter anymore. And I'm not going to say it too loud, but sometimes when she says that, you can tell she wishes it did.

I think we all kind of have our thing that's eating us up out here, you know? When there's nothing but you and other people and darkness and silence, we all look the same. We all get scared sometimes. We all get hungry for something we can't have.

Fimi's been talking about mangoes since the first month we got here. It was annoying at first, but now the way she describes them is almost as good as getting to eat one myself.

I've been picking up some Chinese because Zhang told me that she'd go mad if she couldn't speak to someone in the language she thinks in. I can't quite get the accent right, but she seems to be doing better now that she has someone to talk to.

I'm doing all right myself. The only thing I want up here is you . . . Actually, that's a lie. What I really want is a nice juicy hot dog—like the kind you get at baseball games. Just smothered in onions and mustard, oh man. I'd practically kill for a hot dog, which is really saying something.

Anyway, that's all I got for now.

To the moon and back.

Effie

Hey, Raleigh,

Maritza's teaching me how to play the guitar. She's not that bad once you get past her general irritating personality and figure out how to be asleep when she's awake, but I digress.

We don't have much in common, but she heard me talking to Fimi about Alex and got all excited about her. Apparently, she has a bunch of little sisters and basically helped raise them. So, she started going on and on about how every kid should get a chance to fall asleep to their parent singing and she was adamant about it so I figured I'd take her up on the offer. It's not like I'm going anywhere or anything . . .

So, yeah, she's been teaching me this song and—God, I'm gonna butcher it, but—it's like:

Makochi pitentsin,

Manokoxteka pitelontsin,

makochi kochi noxokoyo.

Manokochteka noxocoyotsin,

manokochteka nopitelontsin.

Yeah.

That's the best I can do now, anyway.

Hope Alex likes it.

To the moon and—*Quit sneaking up on me like that! You guys, it's not funny!*

[other voice: "But you have a beautiful voice!"]

My beautiful voice is a present for my girl, not for you, Gita, damn! I mean, what the hell . . . Get out of the communication room. [mumbled] This soft-headed-ass girl don't know when to quit.

[muffled]

I know you heard that, your ears ain't special.

Okay, sorry about that. Gotta go.

Love you to the moon and back.

Hey, Raleigh,

You won't believe this, but we just passed Jupiter! I got some amazing pictures and the report is gonna be great! Did you know that Jupiter makes sounds? Well, not really, but we have a thing that changes radio emissions to sound waves, but anyway it's fucking wild. Like . . . we turned all the lights off and just sat there listening to it and staring at it 'cause it's so stunning that you really can't do much else. It sounds kind of like if you took a microphone and held it outside during a hurricane. Only it's a bit scarier because it's so close and you can see the atmosphere moving a bit. It was so quiet in this ship it almost felt like church.

Passing Mars's orbit wasn't interesting at all, it was exactly how you imagine it to be and Mars was too far away to get anything good, but Jupiter? Man.

Sometimes I forget why I'm out here—you know, with all the waiting and the bickering that goes on all day. But just . . . wow.

Human eyes, human ears, right? That really is the point of it, and I guess I get why they sent us out here now.

Anyway, I hope you and the kid are all right.

Zhang and Fimi say hi.

Love you to the moon and back.

Effie

[crackling]

Georgina died today.

Astrid . . . found her in the bathroom.

[sniffling]

Raleigh, I don't know why I made this stupid fucking decision. I hate it here. I hate this ship and I hate these people and I hate how fucking dark it is and I totally get it. Georgina gave up and I fucking get it. It took me five years but I finally fucking figured it out.

You know why they sent a bunch of eighteen-year-old kids? Because we're still so stupid, no matter how smart we think we are, we're still dumb as hell and we don't understand things like how long the rest of your life can be. Our brains haven't developed enough to comprehend the magnitude of something like that and they let us . . . sign our lives away just like that.

We don't know what it means to be facing the void with a wall at our backs, we don't know the meaning of words like permanent and forever—we think we do but we don't, we don't know, Raleigh, we don't know!

[crying]

I haven't heard the sound of my mom's voice in years and I can't remember what she sounds like anymore, Raleigh. And from the silence from you I can tell that we've passed the limit from where I can receive your transmissions and I feel like I'm starving. Sometimes the silence is as loud as noise and there's nowhere I can go to run from it.

This is all I have and there's only one way to leave and Georgie fuckin' found it. And God, I would never—you know I would never—but I'm so . . . angry that she—that any of us are even in this position. You can't fucking ask a kid to do something like this and flash things like glory and adventure in her face until she can't see anything but shining lights. It's not fair. It's a trap, and they fucking knew this from the beginning.

I mean. All this . . . it's just rocks! It's just rocks floating around!

I gave up my family for rocks and ice and the

sound of fucking beeping all night long for the rest of my life.

Sending all this shit, all this data back to people who get to go home and raise their own kids and actually live instead of just watching . . .

Because that's what I'm doing.

I'm not living out here, Raleigh, I'm just *out here*.

Hey, Raleigh,

It's been a while. I just . . . wanted to let you know that I'm okay. I'm sorry I didn't send anything for a while, I was just working through some things . . .

Zhang and Maritza got married about a month ago. It was real nice. Everyone was there and Zhang didn't even chew me out over teasing her about calling it years back. It was just really nice to see something new and to see people being happy. You would have cried seeing her face—we all did. Things on the ship seem . . . different now. Better.

I've been thinking about you and the kid a lot lately.

I know I'm not the best, but I want to try to . . . you know, to give her a chance to know me if she wants. I don't know if you play these recordings to her or anything, but I want to talk to her if you can manage it. She must be what, nine? Ten by now?

I want to give her advice and read her stories and sing to her. I want her to know that I still love her. I don't ever want her to question that. Or look up at the sky and think I'm not looking back at her.

Now, I don't know if you married or . . . if you found someone to love you the way you're meant to be loved. And don't for a second think I'm holding you back from that. But you and the kid are it for me.

Raleigh Macallough, you're the love of my life, and I mean to die out here still loving you. I can survive on memories and it's more than enough. I've made peace with that.

I know I'm only twenty-seven, but God, it just . . . feels like it's been so much longer than that.

I really hope you're happy down there. Try to be twice as happy to make up for me.

To the moon and back.

Effie

Hey, kiddo,

My name's Eferhilde, and even though we won't ever see each other again, I still love you very, very much.

Twelve years ago, I decided to leave to do something very important, and I won't be coming back.

Now it might be a bit hard to understand right now, but even though I can speak to you, you can't talk back to me. So if I'm a bit behind on you, or I miss out on teaching you about something, please understand that my words have crossed leagues to reach you.

Right now, I'm somewhere between the orbits of Uranus and Neptune, flying farther and farther away every day. Even though I'm very far, I have many friends where I am, and you shouldn't worry about me.

I just want you to know that I'm here.

Raleigh,

We passed Pluto's orbit today. It's dark and cold and I'm beginning to understand something.

This is all that I am and this is where I am going.

And I think I'm finally okay with it. I think . . . I'm tired enough to become this. To sail past the sunset and watch with human eyes at what lies beyond the horizon.

To the moon and back.

Until the end of time.

Effie

2 HOURS AND 14 MINUTES

The wind whipping against her face barely felt like anything as Ryann drove James and Charlie home. She could only focus on the heat of James at her back and his arms wrapped around her waist.

She stumbled into the house, took off her coat, and sat down at the kitchen table. James brought in the mail, holding Charlie in one arm and a few letters in the other.

He laid the baby down in his crib, then tossed a slim package on the table.

He did the hand gesture that Ryann had learned meant "quick."

The package had the SCOUT logo on it in big white letters. Ryann opened it and pulled out some paperwork.

"They're making me apply like everyone else." Ryann said as she read the documents. "I have to have some sort of applicable skill, so they're sending me to get flying lessons and do some prerequisite courses before announcing I've been accepted."

At least you have a few months before you have to leave, James typed. He put some formula on the stovetop and began stirring it.

"Can I stay in your room tonight?" Ryann asked.

The corner of James's mouth lifted up. *Fine.*

LUSH

The Bird siblings curled close in the dark.

James moved Charlie's crib into his room even though now there was barely any space to open and close the door.

Her name was Adeline, James typed. *I met her in the counseling we had to go to after Mom and Dad died.*

Ryann was suddenly fully awake. She stared up at James, who glanced over at Charlie and nodded.

Her family was a lot more terrible than ours was, even though both of her parents were still around. I liked her because I felt like we had all this sadness in common. We used to hang out before and after counseling, and then more and more.

She was so . . . She wanted a friend who could take care of her and I know that she saw that in me because she told me she did. When we found out about Charlie, she fully expected to take care of him with me. That we could run away together and become a family.

But one day, while at the wellness center, she saw you. I'm not sure what you were doing or how you looked, but she said that she realized that you were taking care of me the way she wanted me to take care of her. And she said that you looked like you were about to fly apart at any moment.

Then she told me that she knew that if she raised Charlie herself, he would be hurt by her parents and her circumstances. But if I raised him, he might actually have a chance. I didn't know if it was that or the pressure of having to be a parent but I trusted her to know her own circumstances. I took him, but I was so scared about what you would do when I walked in the door with him.

"You didn't have to be," Ryann said firmly.

James laughed quietly. *I know. And when you looked at Charlie and at me, then went to go put some blankets in a drawer, I knew that Adeline was right.*

He reached down and brushed his fingers across Ryann's knuckles.

You're the best person I know. But you also would have hunted her down and fought her on sight for adding this to our plates back then, so I did what I had to. Also . . . while I'm on the topic, please don't fistfight anyone in space.

Ryann wiped her face. "I'm not making any promises."

James rolled his eyes.

Do your best, he typed. *Turn this thing into a thing to be proud of. I know you can.*

Ryann nodded against his chest and closed her eyes.

"Birdie. You don't have to talk for me to hear you," she murmured. "Even when it's important, and even though I know that you can. I will always understand."

4 DAYS

Ryann checked the flight-instructor-finder website eight times before deciding she was cursed. She didn't have a ton of time before formal recruitment, so she bit down her pride and headed to the orchard.

Ryann went all the way to the fence at the back and climbed over it and into the apple orchard. She kept walking until she found the main building. Then she took a deep breath and went inside.

It was surprisingly modern, even though she was pretty sure the company was family owned. There were crisp white walls, tasteful steel office decorations, and plush black leather chairs in the waiting area.

The receptionist at the front desk looked up at her impatiently. "May I help you?"

Ryann straightened her shirt and approached the desk. "Hi, is there any way that I can speak to management?"

"This office isn't open to the public. Do you have an appointment?" she snapped.

"No. But I'm willing to wait all day if anyone in charge can spare me five minutes of their time," Ryann said.

The receptionist tightened her lips and picked up the phone. "Mr. Reed, you have a visitor in the lobby, says she'll wait until you're free to talk . . . It's some kid, I don't know." She put the phone down. "Have a seat, he'll be with you shortly."

After about an hour, a tall older man came lumbering down the hallway. He wore a brown twill jumpsuit and black rubber boots, and he had thick gloves folded up in one hand. As soon as he saw Ryann, he waved at her, then turned around and lumbered back the way he came. Ryann glanced over at the receptionist.

"Follow him!" she said, rolling her eyes.

Ryann scrambled up just in time to see the old man turning into an office. When she finally caught up, the old man was sitting in a big oak chair behind a desk. "Have a seat," he said, gesturing at the small chair in front of the desk.

Ryann sat. She opened her mouth to explain why she was there, but the old man interrupted her. "You're that punk who keeps hopping my fence and stealing my apples," he said. "You have anything to say for yourself?"

"I . . . I'm sorry," Ryann stammered. "I shouldn't have trespassed and I shouldn't have taken things that didn't belong to me." She was startled. She'd been doing it for years and thought they hadn't noticed or cared because no one had ever come looking for her.

The old man raised a bristly eyebrow and hummed low in his throat. "Apology accepted," he said, leaning back in his chair. "You look a bit surprised, so I'm assuming you're here for something else. You looking for a job?"

"No," Ryann said. "I . . . know I'm not coming from the best of circumstances and I'm sorry to even be asking, but could you teach me how to fly? You're the only registered flight instructor in thirty miles and I . . ."

Ryann trailed off. The old man was looking at her incredulously, his white eyebrows nearly disappearing into his hairline.

This was a mistake. Coming here was a mistake.

"Never mind," she said, shaking her head and pushing back from the desk. "I'm sorry for taking up your time and for trespassing. I won't do it—"

The old man held up a hand. "Sit. I didn't tell you that you could go."

Then he reached behind himself into a mini fridge next to his desk and pulled out a half-empty jar of Ryann's applesauce and set it on the desk.

Ryann stared at it, horrified.

"When I bought this land," the old man began, "the locals told me I'd have trouble with inventory because it butted up against that trailer park—and they were right, I did. We've been losing crop at the back of this orchard for almost forty years. I chalked it up to maintenance cost and planted a couple rows closer to the office to make up for it. I was more concerned with vandals than anything. Even so, I'm a cautious man, so when the technology allowed for it we put up cameras. When we saw you hop the fence, we didn't look into it. We'd had decades of expecting it. But when you hopped back over and left this, you caught our interest."

He cleared his throat and continued.

"At the time, we weren't sure what was going on, so we dumped it in the trash. The next couple of times we kept the applesauce and sifted through it to see if there was anything wrong with it. Eventually, my granddaughter—the young lady you met when you came in—was brave enough to try it."

He tapped the lid of the jar.

"Forty years people been stealing my apples, and you're the first to give something back. Something so good, you've got my wife trying to replicate it for the holidays." He laughed dryly. "Yours is better by the way. I've always said it's that much sweeter 'cause it's got a little bit of sorry in it."

The old man folded his hands on the desk.

"I'll tell you what. You bring me the recipe for this, and I'll give you what you asked for. It took guts to come in here, and it will take guts to get in the air. Consider yourself two steps ahead. You can call me Reed." He nodded. "Now don't forget to thank Molly on your way out."

12 HOURS

Ryann met Reed the next day, before the sun was all the way up. The old man pocketed her recipe, then took her down to the place his company kept their planes for crop dusting.

They went over basic plane anatomy and some safety rules, then Reed pushed Ryann into the cockpit and settled into the pilot's seat next to her.

"You've gotta feel what you're handling before we do anything else," Reed said. "It's like learning to ride a bike. Once you learn, you don't forget."

They bumped along the ground violently as they rode over gravel and wood chips. Ryann braced herself against the door. Reed looked over at her and chuckled. "Come on now. Don't be a chicken."

They left the ground and Ryann gasped out loud. She half expected them to bang back down to the ground, but the plane sailed smoothly, cresting the apple trees and soaring up over the fields.

Reed laughed at the look on Ryann's face, and she felt a pang at her pride.

"I've never been on a plane before," she admitted.

Reed did that humming in his throat that Ryann noticed

he did when he was unsatisfied, but he didn't say anything to her about it.

He flew them to the edge of the orchard, then turned them back toward the hangar. He settled them to the ground, then hopped out and opened Ryann's door for her. Ryann's legs were shaking and they almost didn't hold her when she stepped down.

Reed helped her the first couple steps, but his face was tight with bewilderment. "If you've never been on a plane before, why are you trying so bad to learn to fly?"

"I need to get somewhere, and this is the only way I can go."

"Can't you just get someone to take you? Jesus, kid, you're white as a sheet."

"No," Ryann said. "I have to do it myself."

Reed nodded, accepting that vague explanation instantly, to Ryann's relief.

"Well. How did it feel?" Reed asked. He pulled off his gloves and shoved them in the front pocket of his jumpsuit.

Ryann thought about it for a minute. "Fast. Dangerous? Limitless," she said finally. "It's hard to be on the ground after feeling so light."

Reed chuckled and clapped Ryann on the back.

3 DAYS

Ryann rode up to the parking gate. The SCOUT building looked very different during the daytime. Less ominous and more . . . like a regular office.

The parking attendant barely glanced at her as she leaned off her motorcycle to scan the brand-new ID. The light turned green, the gate went up, and she pulled into the parking lot.

This time she went through the front door. She passed through a metal detector, then was patted down by a security guard. A young man with bright red hair was waiting by the lobby desk, near the elevators. When he spotted her, he rocked forward on his toes and waved.

Some of the staff watched Ryann curiously as she went down the hallway, but nobody's eyes lingered on her for long. When she got to the elevator, the young man swiped his ID to get in. Then he turned to her. "I'm taking you to medical. Are you a new recruit?"

Ryann nodded.

He smiled and shook her hand. "Wow, you're so lucky! My sister applied last year but they rejected her because she had asthma and flat feet. It's a bit early, so you must be one of the people here on recommendation, huh?"

Ryann looked anxiously around the elevator. It was

packed, but nobody seemed to be paying either of them any attention. "Yeah," she said. "Something like that."

She followed him downstairs to what appeared to be some kind of medical lab with a waiting area up front. He opened another door with his key card, then smiled and stuck out his hand again. "It was nice meeting you. Good luck, and if you see me around, feel free to say hi. My name is Larry."

Ryann nodded and shook his hand. She sat down in a white chair and waited.

An older black woman came into the room and looked at a chart. She called Ryann's name, and Ryann followed her to a back room where they tested her blood pressure and took down her weight and her height. The nurse took several blood samples and then they had her lie down to get scans. They took X-rays and an ultrasound of her chest and pelvis. They did a heart exam and then forced her to run on a treadmill until she couldn't run anymore. Then they collected some of her sweat and a hair sample.

The nurse was very nice. In fact, everyone was very nice. It occurred to Ryann that they might not know why she had been chosen and had no reason to behave differently toward her.

"Did you hear anything about any other recruits?" Ryann tentatively asked the nurse.

The woman thought for a moment. "There's a Swedish girl who should be coming in a couple months from now. She's an exceptional musician and incredibly gifted at . . . something . . . I can't remember. But you're one of the first. You're very lucky you get to come for testing before everyone else."

"What other testing is there?"

"That's a good question," the nurse said. "There's a psych test and another stress test and then a few tests to gauge your basic mathematical skills. Then we'll pull your family history to see if you're at risk for any diseases that would knock you out of qualification. After all that, you get your designation and begin private study. In May, group training begins and you'll move to the dorms with the others if you aren't staying there already."

The nurse glanced at her chart and said, "They list you as being good at mediation and high-stress situations, so they might put you in Psych Eval or Mediation—basically, space human resources." She closed the chart.

Ryann wondered how long they'd been watching her.

Ryann hung up and immediately called Blake. "WHAT THE FUCK, BLAKE?!"

"Hhmwhaa???"

"WHY DID YOU SEND ALEXANDRIA TO MY HOUSE?!"

"She's never been to your house?" Blake slurred. "What time is it? God, I'm so tired. Why is this important?"

"I SPENT THE ENTIRE YEAR MANAGING TO KEEP HER FROM KNOWING WHERE I LIVE AND YOU JUST GIVE IT TO HER LIKE—"

"Dude, it doesn't matter," Blake interrupted. "She's not going to think anything of it, and if she did, she wouldn't be a good friend anyway."

"Fuck you, Blake!"

"You know I'm right—"

Ryann hung up on him.

17 MINUTES

Ryann found Alexandria about five blocks from the trailer park entrance, sitting on a tree stump and playing with her Galaxy Switch.

She stood up when she saw Ryann coming and walked over quickly, like she was about to give Ryann a hug, but she stopped at the last minute and put her Galaxy Switch in her pocket. "Hey. Uh . . . hey," she said nervously. "It's nice to see you."

"Yeah. About that," Ryann said tightly.

"What's wrong?"

"I didn't want you to have to come here," Ryann said.

Alexandria pressed her lips together angrily.

"Not like that—"

"I know what like, Ryann. I did use the map app to get here. I knew where I was going," Alexandria said. "Just be honest with me."

"I'm trying," Ryann said. "I'm trying. But—I don't . . . I didn't want you to see where I live."

"It's getting late," Alexandria said, more gently than Ryann had ever heard her say anything. "Let's go."

They walked until the sidewalk turned into gravel and then gave way to patches of grass, Ryann walking just a bit too quickly for Alexandria to stay next to her. They turned into the park and Ryann could feel Alexandria's gaze heavy on her back and on the homes around them.

Ryann felt like she was seeing it for the first time with her. The homemade, slapdash repairs and some of the trash on the ground, and the kids running around unsupervised in the dead of night. Something in her chest got tight and defensive even though Alexandria hadn't said anything.

When she reached her front door, she went into her pocket to grab her keys, but her hand was shaking so badly that she dropped them. Alexandria quickly grabbed them off the ground and handed them to Ryann, keeping her eyes forward.

Ryann put the key in the door and opened it, and Alexandria followed Ryann into the kitchen.

James looked up at the two of them in undisguised horror. He was sitting at the kitchen table with Charlie in one hand and a bottle in the other. His biology textbook and notes were spread out on the table. His mouth opened and closed soundlessly with shock.

He put the bottle on the table and quickly typed, *Why?*

Ryann just shook her head.

"This is my house," she said to Alexandria. "That's James's son, Charlie." She walked farther in and opened her bedroom door so Alexandria could see it, sheet over the window and all. "This is my room and James's is right over this way. Same layout and everything. The bathroom is around this way . . ."

Alexandria followed her as Ryann gave her a tour of the trailer. Ryann still hadn't looked at her face since she'd met up with her outside.

"It's not much," Ryann said, "but we pay for it ourselves and we always have what we need when we need it. Everyone's been over here, Ahmed and Tomas and Blake and Shannon. We used to have a smaller trailer junior year, but I got this bigger one not that long ago and we're still fixing it up, as you can see—"

"Wow," Alexandria said.

Ryann turned without thinking and accidentally locked eyes with her. "What?" The look on Alexandria's face was one she hadn't seen before and she didn't know what it meant. She could barely hear her over the sound of her heart thudding in her chest.

"I said, 'Wow.' This is amazing. You built a whole life out here all by yourselves? You . . . you're parents?" Alexandria let the words hang while she stared at Charlie and James, who still appeared to be in shock. "I assumed Charlie was your brother." She walked over to the kitchen area and grazed her fingers against the edge of the counter. "Ryann, I didn't . . . You guys must have worked so hard for this," she said.

Charlie began to fuss, so James put him over his shoulder and began to pat his back.

Alexandria turned to James. "I'm sorry for coming over unannounced. Thank you for having me over; your home is beautiful."

James nodded but glanced over at Ryann again for some kind of explanation. Ryann just covered her face with her hands and went back outside.

4 MINUTES

Alexandria came outside and sat down next to Ryann on the stairs.

"James went back to bed," she said. "I don't want to wake him up. Is there anywhere else around here we could talk?"

"You don't have to stay if you don't want to," Ryann said. "It's not—"

"It isn't anything meaningful other than being where you happen to live right now. It's okay," Alexandria said. "Did you really think I'd judge you over this? Stop panicking."

"I can't help it," Ryann said.

Alexandria hummed and leaned back, resting her elbows on the deck. "I came to see you, not your house," she said. "Come on, then. Tell me about how it was at SCOUT."

Ryann sighed. "It's . . . normal feeling. I went in and everyone sort of just . . . told me where to go, and I took some medical tests, kind of like a checkup. Then they let me leave. They have dorms there to stay in but I turned that down."

"Was Roland there?" Alexandria asked. "Did you have to talk to him again?"

"No," Ryann said. "I asked, but the nurse said he barely comes out of his office when he's there unless some special project or an event happens."

Alexandria snorted. "Do you think we were a special project or an event?"

"Both. Definitely both." Ryann laughed.

"Wow. High praise." Alexandria grinned. She gazed at the sky. "They're probably watching us," she murmured.

Ryann stuck her middle finger up at the sky. "You know I'm kidding," she said loudly. "But the sentiment is still there, you dicks."

Alexandria giggled and spread her arms out behind her head. "This is so dumb and weird."

"Yeah. I'm starting to phase out of the horrified disassociation phase into the casual acceptance with a few drops of hysteria phase," Ryann admitted.

"That's a good place to be," Alexandria said softly.

28 MINUTES

They took a walk down by the orchard, along the fence where there was an overgrown trail and the air smelled like spring and old fruit.

Alexandria lit their path with her phone until their eyes adjusted to the darkness. Ryann recounted her SCOUT visit in as much detail as she could.

Alexandria let Ryann talk until she had no more to say, then they settled into a comfortable silence.

"What was that first night like?" Alexandria finally asked.

"Which?"

"The first night you sat on my roof?"

Ryann grinned. "Well. It was more boring than the ones after it. You left all your stuff in a mess so I cleaned it up. Then I just kind of lay there and struggled against going into your room and snooping around."

Alexandria laughed. "I'd be mad at that comment, but your house is immaculate. We have very different definitions of clean."

Ryann hmmed. Alexandria's hand swung next to her emptily, and Ryann itched to grab it.

"I looked up at the sky and wondered if that was what it

felt like to be you," Ryann admitted. "I didn't know you back then. I couldn't have known, but I think I wasn't too off the mark."

"You deserve to go. You always have," Alexandria said suddenly. "I came because I needed you to know that. You're very self-deprecating and I need you to leave without questioning this. The instant he offered, I knew that I couldn't go. That's what I was crying about, not about meeting him or anything. It's inevitable to me, but I still wanted time to mourn it."

Ryann stopped in her tracks. "Why?"

Alexandria sighed and ran her fingers through her hair. It was more black than blond now and was messier and more her than Ryann had ever seen it.

"I can't leave my dad alone in that house," she said plainly. "I can't take the last thing he has away from him."

Ryann tilted her head to the side and considered Alexandria. "You asked me to be selfish. Couldn't you have been selfish as well?"

"I wanted to," Alexandria whispered. "God, I wanted to. But I have to break the cycle. I have to do it, just like you have to go: Because this might be the only chance you'll ever have. This is my only chance, too."

Alexandria reached up and placed her hand on Ryann's

shoulder, then cupped the back of Ryann's neck. "You're so strong . . . ," she said. "That will help you up there, I think."

Ryann swallowed tightly and leaned down, but Alexandria pulled away, crossing her arms over her chest.

"Do . . . you want to stay?" Ryann asked. "It's too late to really walk around here now—things get dodgy around two a.m. and who knows if your dad will be—"

"You don't have to think up excuses," Alexandria said, turning back the way they came. "I'll stay."

2 HOURS

There was enough space between them for Ryann to be able to stretch her arm out completely and still not touch Alexandria. She was curled up facing the wall, but she wasn't asleep yet. Ryann stared at her back and tried to stop wanting to touch her.

"I wasn't sure I would get to see you again," Ryann whispered, the darkness and silence making her bold.

Alexandria was quiet for a minute, then she turned over on her back. Shifting a couple inches nearer.

"One day, you won't," Alexandria said plainly.

They breathed into the quiet for what felt like hours, until Alexandria turned back onto her side and faced the wall.

"Don't—" Ryann started, then paused. "Don't forget about me."

Alexandria didn't reply.

7 HOURS AND 8 SECONDS

They woke up back to back. Identical apostrophes in the warmth of Ryann's bed.

Alexandria sat up first and Ryann looked over at her, sitting there, bleary eyed with the sun illuminating her bright hair. They locked eyes for an eon before Ryann had to close her gaze against the sight. Alexandria escaped to go brush her teeth.

Ryann went through the day on autopilot. Unable to shake the memory of Alexandria's back pressed against her and the wheezy soft sound she made as she slept.

3 DAYS AND 6 HOURS

Ryann liked Reed. He was straightforward and firm.

Reed expected her there every day before the sun was completely up on the days they had a flying lesson. He expected Ryann to remember exactly what he'd taught her the last time, and he expected Ryann to be able to repeat it on command.

He let her steer in the air for a week before setting her in the pilot's seat and making her practice taking off and landing. By the time they started actually flying, Ryann was almost impatient to do it.

Reed chuckled and nodded the final time he made Ryann land immediately instead of accelerate into the air.

"If you're busy being hotheaded, you won't have time to be nervous," he explained, his eyes twinkling.

Ryann sighed theatrically as Reed laughed louder.

"Don't get your britches all wound up. You're coming along just fine. Now put some fire under that ass and get to training. Don't make me make you late."

8 DAYS

The first time Ryann crested the trees, she smiled so wide her face felt like it was splitting.

"Now we're talking!" Reed shouted, and clapped loudly. "And ain't it a beauty! Aw, quit grinning so wide, you'll outshine the sun."

Ryann laughed and felt freer than she had in months.

"She laughs, too?" Reed joked. "Well, I'll be."

Ryann gazed out into the sky as the morning turned from pink to blue, and she sailed until she could tread the wind like waves. Reed beamed next to her the whole time.

When Ryann gently drifted them back to the ground and into the hangar, Reed shook his head in delight and patted her on the back again. Ryann was sure her shoulder was getting bruised.

"We do that a couple dozen more times and you'll be good to take your exam, no problem," Reed assured her. "You'll be a pilot before you get your high school diploma, if I have anything to do with it. Let me know when you do so we can celebrate."

"Actually, can I ask a favor of you? For if I pass the test?"

"Sure kid, what do you need?"

3 WEEKS

The day before Ryann went over state lines to take her flight exam, Alexandria decided that they should go sit on the roof one last time for old time's sake. They waited until midnight, then snuck Ryann in through the back door—closing it softly and running up the stairs.

Ryann lifted Alexandria up through the skylight, even though her arm had been healed for ages. Then she lay in her old spot and looked up at the stars.

"They seem close," Ryann observed.

"They aren't," Alexandria replied.

"They're closer now that they've ever been, technologically speaking. They'll be closer soon when we learn how to get to them even faster," Ryann said. She reached across the shingles separating them and linked her pinkie with Alexandria's. "Remember a few months ago, when we were walking in the woods by the warehouse, I was telling you about wanting to go into space and not really thinking that I could? Then you looked at me and said you really thought I could?" Ryann asked.

Alexandria huffed mirthlessly. "Famous last words. Yes, I remember."

"You . . . you gotta try."

"Try what?"

"Try to find me. Someday."

Alexandria leaned over and her face eclipsed light-years from Ryann's view.

"That's a tall order, Ryann Bird," she whispered.

"You're the tallest person I know." Ryann grinned.

Alexandria laughed and Ryann knew it would be something she wouldn't have to learn to miss.

3 DAYS

Ryann mailed her flight exam results to SCOUT. Then she stared up at the sun and thought about how daytime didn't exist in space.

5 HOURS

"Are you sure this is okay?" Alexandria frowned and touched the outside of the plane.

"Reed said that if I passed the exam, I was allowed to take someone up unsupervised," Ryann said.

"At night?" Alexandria looked at the cockpit forebodingly.

Ryann rolled her eyes. "Yes, at night. That's like an entire part of the exam. Just get in. I pinkie promise I won't kill you."

Alexandria scowled but she got in and closed the door. When Ryann turned on the plane, Alexandria jumped.

"You had to have flown to move here," Ryann said. "Literally, what is wrong?"

"I don't know. It's . . . bumpier," Alexandria said.

"Yeah. It won't be for long, though." Ryann drove them down the orchard runway. She glanced over at Alexandria, who was clutching the side of the plane tightly. "Ready?"

"No."

The plane lifted off the ground—effortless and smooth—but Alexandria yelped anyway. Ryann coasted over the trees and arced off into the indigo sky.

"It's okay," she said. "You can open your eyes."

Alexandria reached over and gripped Ryann's wrist tightly.

"That's . . . an interesting way of letting me control whether or not this goes safely," Ryann said dryly. "Open your eyes, you're missing the best part. You can't see a view like this from a commercial plane."

Alexandria did, then she slammed them shut again.

"You want to go back down," Ryann said, disappointed.

Alexandria didn't say anything.

"Okay," Ryann sighed. "Okay."

21 MINUTES AND 3 SECONDS

Ryann landed the plane in a clearing in the middle of the road not far from the hangar. She hopped out of the plane, then went over to the other side and opened Alexandria's door. She was still shaking, so Ryann reached in and helped her gently down to the ground.

"It's safe," Ryann said. "I'd never do anything to hurt you. You know that?"

Alexandria took a deep breath and steadied herself on the side of the plane. "I know," she replied.

Ryann squeezed her arm. "You stay here. I'm going to drive the plane back, then I'll take you home."

17 MINUTES

The ride back was quiet.

Alexandria had stopped shaking and had buried her face into the back of Ryann's neck, resting her chin on the collar of Ryann's leather jacket.

Ryann pulled her bike into the back of Alexandria's house slowly, trying to keep the noise down so Mr. Macallough wouldn't wake up.

"I'm sorry," Ryann said as Alexandria got off.

Alexandria didn't respond, but she made a soft sound. Ryann turned around in alarm.

Alexandria was crying.

"It's not your fault," she sniffled. "It's not the plane . . . not really."

Ryann gently took the helmet out of Alexandria's hands and turned off her bike. "I wanted to do something fun and show you what I learned," she explained quietly.

"Why are you doing this to me, though?" Alexandria said.

"I . . . I wanted to give you a chance to fly," Ryann said. "Or at least to fly with me at least once before—"

"No," Alexandria said firmly, shaking her head once. "Not that. Why are you trying to make me love you before you have to go?"

Ryann didn't say anything. She couldn't. Somehow, even though she'd thought that word for months, hearing it out of Alexandria's mouth like this—after all this—was somehow great and also terrible.

Alexandria moved her hand from Ryann's arm, to her shoulder, to her neck, to her cheek. Ryann clenched Alexandria's wrist and felt her bones grind beneath her fingers, and Alexandria gripped her jaw so tight Ryann was sure it would bruise.

"Why do you keep looking at me and touching me when you know that I fully understand the price of losing that?" Alexandria whispered. "Why are you ripping me open every day when I'm trying so hard to patch myself closed?

"It was going to be easy, I was just going to grow up alone and leave. But then you kicked your way into my life and threw your fragile friends in front of me and now I am tearing out pieces of myself to try to figure out how to get back to where I started.

"I spent months trying to unlearn loving you, trying to forget the strength of your hands and the worlds in your eyes. But there is no part of me left that you have not touched. We just spent forever finding out what it meant to have one foot out in the heliosphere and the other here on Earth, testing just how far a heart can stretch. I heard it in her voice, how much it hurts, and I am terrified that same thing will kill me.

"Why are you rebuilding the tragedy that built me?" It was a question, and a threat.

Ryann squeezed her eyes tight and said the thing that had hidden behind her teeth for months. "Because I had to. Because I'm selfish. Because I want you more than I care about whether it hurts us or not."

Alexandria laughed. "I never—You never stop surprising me—"

Ryann stole the rest of whatever Alexandria was going to say beneath the press of her lips. Alexandria pushed Ryann back against her bike, scrambling her hands beneath Ryann's jacket and shirt so she could feel her skin.

"You're an asshole, Ryann Bird," Alexandria said between gasps. "You made me wait until the last fucking minute for this."

"I'm sorry, I'm sorry." Ryann laughed into Alexandria's slender neck, biting it sweetly. "You're scary. I . . . I didn't know. I didn't want to—" She recaptured Alexandria's lips, framing her face with trembling hands. Alexandria leaned in close, peeling Ryann's jacket off her shoulders as she leaned in.

Ryann's bike jerked under their weight and then turned on its side, dumping them unceremoniously onto the gravel.

Alexandria turned on her back, spread out on the filthy rocks, and laughed loudly. Ryann's eyes tingled with tears and she buried her face in the crook of Alexandria's shoulder.

"Okay. Fuck. Well. It's way too late to sneak in the front door, so let's climb the trellis and go in through the roof," Alexandria said, curling an arm around Ryann's neck. "All we ever do is break into places."

Ryann snorted and kissed Alexandria gently on the cheek.

8 MINUTES

Alexandria closed the skylight and climbed down to the floor. She walked across the room and turned off the light, then she came and stood in front of Ryann, gazing up at her.

"Four light-years from the second largest pulsar, past the black dust and the white. In a small circle of golden light, made by a careful teenage star, I found you," Alexandria said seriously. "No matter what I did or said, there you stood. Like a fixed point, and the Earth moved around you."

"Everything you say is like poetry," Ryann whispered.

"Is that what made you love me?"

"No," Ryann said hoarsely. "On the first day . . . Even on the first day, you were so angry and luminous and demanding. You looked like . . . the whole world was built just so that you could walk on it. Who could look away from that? Who would want to?"

Alexandria held Ryann's face in her hands and Ryann exhaled softly, swaying forward.

"Four months ago . . . when I saw you waiting at the top of that hill," Alexandria said, "I learned what it meant to be hungry for you. I learned what it meant to make peace with starving. You want to see space? I've been staring at it in your eyes for months. You want to leave? I've spent all year learning what it means to endure. I know the weight of this and I know the price."

Alexandria grazed her lips over Ryann's forehead, nose, and cheeks, then kissed her so softly it was barely a taste of breath. "This is the most human thing I know," she said. "I need you to take it with you." She squeezed Ryann's neck and then led her backward to her bed.

Ryann gasped as Alexandria lay her down. "How is this real? It doesn't feel real."

"I'm here. Let me show you."

9 HOURS AND 15 SECONDS

The next morning, Ryann woke up in Alexandria's bed.

Alexandria's bed was harder than Ryann remembered, but she was warm from the sunlit window and Alexandria lying next to her. She curled up on her side and pulled the pillow from the headboard to hold it happily. When she did, something crinkled quietly. She reached underneath and pulled out a paper crane.

Not a paper crane, she realized, *her* paper crane.

Her crane with Alexandria's notes on the back that she'd tossed off the roof like trash because she could always make more. The crane that she made weeks before she could even remotely have called Alexandria her friend.

Ryann stared at it, her heart banging in her chest.

Alexandria turned over and blinked awake slowly.

"The crane," Ryann said, voice rough from sleep.

Alexandria gazed at Ryann holding it for a while, then closed her eyes again.

"I was so afraid that it would get wet sitting on the lawn that I went downstairs to pick it up after you left," Alexandria said softly. "I didn't want to lose it."

"Mmm. I'll make you as many as you like."

"I . . . already knew how to make them," Alexandria admitted. "I just wanted you to . . . I didn't know you were capable of something so delicate. I didn't know you then and I was surprised and I . . . wanted something that we had in common."

Ryann laughed. She laughed until Alexandria pushed her out of the bed in angry embarrassment, then she hopped up, straddled Alexandria's lap, and kissed her all over her face until Alexandria pushed her out of the bed again.

Ryann's phone dinged and she scooped it off the desk.

"Ahmed says 'Congratulations.' I told him that I was taking you out to fly and he just assumed . . . He's good at that. He also said that if we wanted to swing with him and Shannon they're open to that. Side note—we're not doing that."

Alexandria scowled and turned bright red.

"He also said that we should make a bucket list of things we want to do before I go."

Alexandria looked pensive. "I . . . I . . . Would you . . . Would you go to prom with me? I want to go with you."

"No," Ryann said.

Alexandria looked crestfallen.

"At homecoming they ran out of things to drink and

I'm not drinking out of a faucet again," Ryann said resolutely. "But I will dance with you. I want to dance with you at least once."

She texted Ahmed quickly and rolled back under the blankets to sleep longer.

1 DAY

After school, Ryann swung by Mrs. Marsh's classroom. They hadn't had any meetings since Ryann and Alexandria had their fight, months and months ago. Mrs. Marsh hadn't asked her to come by, or asked about Alexandria since she saw them hanging up posters with Shannon in the hallway and accurately assumed that they'd figured things out.

So when she saw Ryann knocking on her door, she looked appropriately confused, but she got up and opened it.

"You're lucky I'm still here. I thought things were going well these days," Mrs. Marsh said, tossing on her jacket. "You having trouble in paradise?"

Ryann grinned wryly. "No . . . not that. I just came to say good-bye."

Mrs. Marsh was shoving folders into her bag, but she looked up at that in confusion.

"Good-bye for what?" she said.

"I'm . . . dropping out to—" Ryann started.

"YOU'RE DROPPING . . . WHAT? WE HAVE TWO WHOLE MONTHS LEFT OF CLASS. WHAT ABOUT PROM?"

"I'm dropping out to go train for SCOUT. I'm going to space. I'm dropping out of high school so I can go to space,

Mrs. Marsh. Also, Alexandria is my girlfriend now. Or at least she is until I go to space. So I came here to say good-bye and to say thank you."

"Holy shit!" Mrs. Marsh blurted.

Ryann chuckled. "Yeah, it's been a while and a lot of things have happened and I'm just catching you up on—"

"Holy shit," Mrs. Marsh repeated. "What . . . the fuck. What kind of cinematic . . . who . . . who does that? What kind of enchanted . . . How did you even . . . Oh my God." She leaned heavily against her desk and took in a huge gulp of air and let it out in a whoosh.

"Yeah," Ryann said. "You look really pale, are you okay?"

"I am . . . something. Your girlfriend? Really? How . . . did you manage that?" Mrs. Marsh shook her head to clear it. "Not that I didn't think—and you're a very nice young lady so this isn't a shot at that, but—"

"She likes my muscles," Ryann said, deadpan. "And I tricked her into it by flying her on a plane until she was too dizzy to say no."

Mrs. Marsh grew even paler. "You flew a plane . . ."

"Hmm," Ryann said, with growing concern. "Let's focus on my good-bye before wherever your blood seems to be going gets any more crowded."

"Yeah." Mrs. Marsh nodded like a bobblehead, clearly

still processing this information. "Okay, yeah. Can I hug you? You don't look like the hugging type but I'd like to."

Ryann grinned, wrapped her arms around Mrs. Marsh, and squeezed her tight. She pretended she didn't hear her sniffling.

"You're a great teacher," she said. "Thanks for being there."

"I'm a great matchmaker, too. And post-secondary education advisor," Mrs. Marsh said wetly into the shoulder of Ryann's jacket.

"Yeah. That, too."

The sun lit up Alexandria's white-blond tipped hair in shades of pink and orange as she drove them down the street. Neither of them said anything, but it was a warm quiet, not a cold one. Ryann thought about the reckless drive Alexandria had taken her on earlier in the year and how easily she'd been convinced that Alexandria just drove that way regularly.

Alexandria drove to suit her mood, she realized. They were coasting like a calm sea.

This was so different. The more she thought about it, everything was so different now. She hadn't planned for this year to go this way. She was sure she'd be a little unhappier. Maybe get in a little more trouble than usual. Graduate with a minimum of a 1.5 GPA and maybe join the military if nowhere around here hired for decent pay.

Now she was riding down the road with this feeling in her chest.

With a full understanding of how good things can be and how temporary.

Alexandria glanced away from the road for a second, feeling Ryann's eyes on her, but Ryann didn't look away.

It finally didn't feel like she needed to.

THE LAST DAY

Ryann wore her dad's suit, the one she'd wanted to wear for the winter formal that Shannon had talked her out of. She went to pick up Alexandria, who shimmied down the trellis in an iridescent slip of a dress and her regular gym shoes.

Alexandria hopped on Ryann's bike and put on her helmet. She tucked her hands into the pockets of Ryann's suit as she gripped Ryann's waist tight.

Blake had set up two speakers in the warehouse. Shannon had taken some of the decorations she'd used while on prom committee and tucked streamers up around the walls and taped balloons around the room.

There were more people there than Ryann had thought there would be. She'd assumed that only a few would have come—maybe some of Shannon's friends or Blake's cast members from his most recent play. But there were at least fifty other kids from school there, too, dancing and eating the snacks Shannon had brought.

Alexandria tucked her small hand in Ryann's larger one and beamed brightly by her side as Ryann made her way over to Ahmed.

Ahmed was dancing with Shannon, but when he spotted Ryann walking over, he snatched himself out of Shannon's grip, whirled around, and hugged Ryann tightly. Shannon immediately glommed on to the back of the hug, wrapping her arms clean around Ahmed's body to cling onto Ryann with her fingertips. Ryann could hear Alexandria laughing behind her and she felt Alexandria's cheek press into the center of her spine.

Tomas slammed into them from the right side, yelling, "I hate you for leaving."

"He doesn't hate you." Blake steadied the group hug from the left so they all didn't fall in a pile.

"I know," Ryann said. She freed one of her arms so she could wrap it around Tomas's neck.

"This was fun at first, but it's not fun anymore," Ahmed said. He began to wriggle free, predictably unable to handle any hug longer than a few seconds, so they all peeled off until Ahmed was free.

"Where's James?" Ryann asked. She'd left him with Tomas so she could pick up Alexandria.

Ahmed shrugged, adjusting his suit. "I don't know, in the corner maybe?"

Ryann turned around and found Tomas lifting Charlie out of James's arms so he could sway Charlie to the music. Ryann scowled. She whipped out her phone and texted Tomas.

Ryann: Get him home by 9pm or we'll have problems.

Tomas glanced down at his phone and then across the room at Ryann. He gave her a peace sign and then continued what he was doing.

Ryann: Tomas, so help me God—

Ryann typed, but then Alexandria put a hand on her arm.

"He loves him; it will be okay," she said. "You owe me a dance."

Ryann never liked dancing much. She lacked a natural rhythm and no one had ever asked her to dance because she was always so much taller than anyone else.

But Alexandria didn't ask much of her.

She just wrapped her arms around Ryann's neck and swayed her side to side.

"Thank you for making this easy for me," Ryann whispered.

Alexandria laughed full and open, then rested her forehead against Ryann's collarbone.

"No really, I've never slow danced with anyone before," Ryann said seriously.

"Why not?" Alexandria asked.

Ryann shrugged self-consciously. "I don't think anyone wanted to. With me."

"I want to," Alexandria said. "I always will."

3 HOURS, 18 MINUTES, AND 47 SECONDS

Tomas took James and Charlie home like he promised. He got back just in time to join everyone in cleaning up the warehouse. Blake had already packed his speakers back in his car, but he had come back in to sweep up all the confetti and popped balloons. Ahmed was helping Ryann stack chairs in the corner while Shannon and Alexandria gathered up all the trash.

Ryann rolled her shoulders to loosen them, then began dragging the chairs outside to Tomas's parents' van. When she came back inside, Ahmed and Tomas were standing by the radio, looking shocked.

Alexandria dropped the trash bag she was holding and sprinted across the warehouse. She wrenched the volume up, and the room filled with Eferhilde Watts's warm, rich voice echoing from six billion miles away.

"—*Age, both wondrous and quite simple after all. And in this place of noise and silence, of light and darkness, of family and loneliness, of death and life, all that we are is humanity.*

"*All that I am is a terribly brave small thing, with a terribly brave small life, and a terribly brave love that spans eons.*

"*All that you are is the tether to that love—as timeless and brilliant as the night sky.*

"And all Alexandria is, is the very last thing I did before I turned into a brave small thing, and she's bigger than the both of us combined, I bet.

"As we step out into the black, as far and wide as hope, and take steps that will always be humanity's first, I am reminded that I no longer have to wonder, or look back at what was left behind. Because I know who and what I am, and I know where I am going. And I know that when I finally get there, you'll be coming to join me.

"Because we'll always wind up at the same place when the sun goes down for good, Raleigh.

"We are all together in this incomprehensible wait."

The wind blew warm and strong through the skylight, buffeting against them with the strength of an oncoming storm.

"Wow," Ahmed whispered, his dark eyes glittering. "I think I get it now."

8 MONTHS

Ryann tightened her tie and ran a nervous hand over her shaved head.

Training had gone as well as expected, she supposed. She was svelte and angular now. She was ready.

Ryann tucked her white shirt into her dress pants and slipped her leather jacket on over her suit. She wouldn't be allowed to take it with her, but she wanted her friends to see her in it one last time. So they could keep that memory.

Brigitte, her dorm roommate, watched as she got ready. "You look good," she said. "Like a boy, but a pretty one."

Ryann huffed a laugh at that. "I don't think Alexandria will mind."

She closed her room door behind her and headed down the hallway. Ryann turned past the library and reflexively glanced inside. Roland's office door was open a crack. She thought about going in to speak with him, but decided against it.

She scanned her ID and took the elevator up to the first floor.

"She's always late," she heard James say. "She doesn't bother to hurry. I always told her it was super rude, but whatever. It's not like *I* know anything about—"

James stopped talking.

Ryann stared at them.

James had dyed back his hair to brown from purple and was holding Tomas's hand.

That was new.

Charlie was standing all by himself. Blake had a tight grip on the back of his overalls as Charlie strained to get away.

Shannon had chopped her golden ringlets into a bob, but she still beamed like sunlight.

Ahmed was six inches taller, evidently having hit a long-awaited growth spurt after graduation.

Alexandria . . . had shaved her head. Her face was just as sharp and lovely as the first time Ryann had seen it.

Ryann let out a breath and tried to crystallize this image in her mind.

James crashed into her like a freight train, dragging Tomas with him as he screamed her name. Ahmed, Shannon, and Blake followed close behind, adding to the pile. Ryann kissed Charlie and held him close, even as he wriggled in her arms and babbled new words she'd never gotten to hear him learn.

Ahmed whispered to her about the ring he was planning to give Shannon and Ryann punched him in the arm one last time for old-time's sake. Tomas blubbered into her shoulder worse than James was doing and said a bunch of chaotic things about robbing the cradle, so Ryann gave her blessing to all that. Blake smacked Ryann in the shoulder, then crumpled and hugged her tight. When he pulled back his eyes were wet. He blinked until that wasn't happening anymore.

"We have the same haircut," he observed, rubbing Ryann's head. "It looks good, you lady killer."

Alexandria hung back from the others and waited for Ryann to come to her instead.

Ryann took off her jacket and wrapped it around Alexandria's shoulders. Tomas hooted obnoxiously in the background and clapped.

Ryann pulled Alexandria close by the collar and closed her eyes, pressing their foreheads together. Alexandria sighed and linked both their pinkies together, then closed her eyes, too.

Ryann smirked. "You gonna kiss me or are we just going to stand here?"

Alexandria opened her eyes. "Nah. I'm sure you'll get by without it," she said.

Ryann groaned. "Hideously mean to the very last. Come here."

Ryann kissed Alexandria on the forehead and on both cheeks and on the tip of her nose, then wrapped her so tight she was sure she'd squeezed a few tears out.

Alexandria cupped Ryann's face close and said, "I'll be coming for you. This might be your one shot, but it's not mine. We are better and smarter than they were, and we have more time. I'll find a way, and then I'm coming for you."

When the time came, she was ready.

Ryann Bird walked the hall of ages: from the gates of man to the arches of the gods, and thought about what it meant to be Ryann Bird.

She gazed at Marija's nape in front of her and wondered who Marija's Alexandria was. Whether Marija missed them like a burn and felt the time between them stretching . . .

Omotunde placed a blue-black hand on Ryann Bird's shoulder and squeezed. Ryann looked back at her, found the same wonder-terror in her blue-black eyes. She saw herself reflected, at the end of all things. Framed in the portrait of Omotunde's eyelashes as they stood there together, made of all the same things.

"If you cannot walk, we will carry you," Omotunde said.

Ryann kept walking, because she already knew.

Crews typically joke and banter a bit, the atmosphere is lighthearted, during the short drive to the launch pad. Everyone falls silent as the bird comes into view.

She is beautiful. She is ready, as are we.

Leroy Chiao
May 9, 2009

Anyone who sits on top of the largest hydrogen-oxygen-fueled system in the world, knowing they're going to light the bottom, and doesn't get a little worried, does not fully understand the situation.

John Young

1981

And so it's a very gentle liftoff, contrary to what most people think when they see all the fire and smoke of launch . . . Then just insertion into orbit, and that's where the highest strain on the body is, about seven, almost eight Gs at that time.

John Glenn
2012

The liftoff occurs . . . The shuttle's acceleration is so great, the force is so tremendous—the raw acceleration is so hard to describe! At the very least, you know you are going somewhere, and that somewhere is up, very quickly.

John Mace Grunsfeld
April 25, 2011

The vehicle shakes and vibrates, and you are pinned hard down into your seat by the acceleration. As one set of engines finishes and the next starts, you are thrown forward and then shoved back.

Chris Hadfield
December 13, 2012

In the last couple of minutes, we actually have to throttle the main engines back to maintain the three Gs on the vehicle and on our bodies, because the rocket just wants to keep going faster and faster, and it would end up tearing the rocket apart.

Mike Good
July 8, 2011

It was the sound of immense power unleashed in barely controlled fury.

Pat Pilcher

July 26, 2016

I realized that all the training we'd had on what to do if something went wrong during launch—how to bail out, how to operate the parachutes, how to make an emergency landing—I realized that all those years of training were completely pointless. It was just filler to make us feel okay about climbing into this thing. Because if it's going down, it's going down.

Michael J. Massimino

2016

I wasn't really scared. I was very excited, and I was very anxious.

Sally Ride
1998

*And then suddenly we were weightless, Raleigh! I
looked out the window and thought: On this rock
where we were all born, with its oceans and its
seas and its muskrats and its pomelos and its diamonds and its viruses and its books and its dust as
old as time—small quivering things packaged up
their hope and their curiosity. They buried it in the
bones of their girl children, precious and valuable
as we are. They took our bodies and strapped them
into ships they took twenty million years to learn to
build. They tore pieces of our Earth from the deep-
est reaches and used it to safely bind our bodies
in place. They melted the sands the waves beat on
the shores so our small faces could be protected.
They stole lightning from the skies so we could fly.*

Eferhilde Watts

2010

372

In the quiet of all that space, everything mattered and nothing really did. The other girls were smart and we trusted one another, and as we were tossed back and forth in the fray it was good to know that we weren't alone.

Ryann Bird

2028

19 YEARS

Ryann finished making her coffee and headed down to Communications. She slid into one of the terminals and booted up the receiver. She uploaded the reports about the health and well-being of her crewmates and sent the documents to SCOUT, like she did on the last day of every month.

Then she opened up her messages. She had a new form to be reviewed, which she transferred to her datapad to read in her room later.

There was another message, an audio one starred with *Urgent,* which was concerning, because the last time they'd all gotten a message starred as urgent they were being warned about potential weaknesses in the original ship design. It had been a harrowing issue, but engineering was resourceful and they'd made it past the problem without losing any lives. That was only three months ago though—easily enough time for the repairs to have failed—so Ryann's heart was in her throat as she opened up the transmission.

I'm coming.

Ryann dropped her mug and it shattered on the Communications floor.

I don't know if you're okay or if you met anyone else up there, but made a pinkie promise and you know how I feel about those. Sorry it's been a while. School takes a long-ass time as you know . . . or, well, you don't know, but I literally had to get a doctorate before NASA would draft me. Then, they only wanted people with engineering experience, so I had to get another doctorate.

Anyway. We're faster now, at least three times as fast as the ship you're on. So technically, if we did the math right—and holy shit do we need to make sure the math is right . . . , Alexandria whispered, slightly away from the microphone, *I could be there in two, maybe three years?*

As romantic as it would be, I'm not just coming to kiss your stupid face. We're bringing supplies and raw materials to help update the ship. Then, if you're not too dazzled by the stars and if you're way more dazzled by my pretty face, we could . . . go home maybe? It would take another four years, but what's four more years after all this? Ryann could hear the smile in Alexandria's voice. She covered her face with her hands and cried.

I know we haven't spoken since you passed Jupiter and I couldn't catch your radio waves anymore, but I . . . still want to see you. So. Wait for me. I'm coming. Pinkie promise.

AUTHOR'S NOTE

There are many things I wish I hadn't done. There are many places I wish I hadn't gone, things I wish I hadn't said, risks that weren't worth the risk. Part of being a person is making choices, and part of making choices is taking responsibility for the results, if that choice turns out to be a mistake.

Ryann and Alexandria were born to inherit the mistakes of those that came before them. Most of us are.

But what we do with those mistakes—both our own and those we inherit—can mean the difference between prolonged suffering and the chance to grow beyond our circumstances.

Roland's mistake was so large that it eclipsed the mistakes of nearly everyone in the book, and left everyone he touched in the darkness of the shadow of his failure.

Eferhilde's choices left the ones she loved shivering and exposed, buffeted by strong winds of loss.

Raleigh's emotional neglect made his home empty and cold, while he desperately craved warmth and connection.

Each of them pushed away regret, stretched their rejection of being wrong over years, holding so tightly to their pain that it became an inseparable part of them. Then when it was time to make peace, they had to be dragged toward it kicking and screaming—Roland by Alexandria, Raleigh by Ryann, and Eferhilde by the yawning void of eternity before her.

I filled The *Weight Of The Stars* with teenagers throttling their trauma instead of drowning in it because you deserve to see your peers being strong. I gave you:

James and his baby, whom he speaks to after months of silence.

Tomas, who beat addiction and self-loathing and stands proudly on the ashes of what was.

Blake, who loves and loves and loves in his own way, because he knows people need it.

Shannon, who saw the ghost of a rejected brother in the rejected kids at school and sat down beside them.

Ahmed, who knows that choosing loyalty is as serious as life and death.

Alexandria, who learned to hold people close instead of pushing them away.

And Ryann, my wildest child, who clenches joy and hope in each fist.

They are, all of them, running toward the sun.

Please look at them and know that you too can seize your failure by the neck and look it in the eyes. Know that you can gaze at the you that was and say, "I love you. You can be more than this."

Know that you can step forward, even when everything in you is screaming to keep looking back.

You are evolving and growing.

You deserve to.

Love,
Kayla

ACKNOWLEDGMENTS

This book is an ode to the amazing WLW community that turned out in droves to support *The Wicker King*; a tiny, strange book from a tiny, strange girl, produced by everyone on a huge leap of faith. I saw your fan works and your tears and saw you begging people to read me and was touched beyond belief. I built this sweetness for you. You all deserve good things. You all deserve happy endings.